Candy Canes, Canines & Crime

A Dickens & Christie Large
Print Mystery
Book VIII

Kathy Manos Penn

Paperback ISBN: 979-8-9855140-4-9

eBook ISBN: 979-8-9855140-3-2

Large Print: 979-8-9855140-5-6

This book is for my father and the cats and dogs he loved. How appropriate that his last dog was named Noel because he brought her home one holiday season.

Dogs do speak, but only to those who know how to listen.

- Orhan Pamuk

Contents

CAST OF CHARACTERS   IX

CHAPTER ONE   1

CHAPTER TWO   27

CHAPTER THREE   37

CHAPTER FOUR   53

CHAPTER FIVE   71

CHAPTER SIX   93

CHAPTER SEVEN   123

CHAPTER EIGHT   145

CHAPTER NINE   167

CHAPTER TEN   203

CHAPTER ELEVEN   223

CHAPTER TWELVE   251

CHAPTER THIRTEEN   285

CHAPTER FOURTEEN   311

CHAPTER FIFTEEN   327

CHAPTER SIXTEEN   341

Please take a minute   355

Books mentioned in Candy Canes,   360
Canines & Crime

About the Author   363

Also By Kathy Manos Penn   366

CAST OF CHARACTERS

The Americans

Aleta "Leta" Petkas Parker—A retired American banker, Leta lives in the village of Astonbury in the Cotswolds with Dickens the dog and Christie the cat. Nicknamed Tuppence.

Henry Parker—Handsome blue-eyed Henry was Leta's husband.

Anna Metaxas—Leta's youngest sister lives in Atlanta with her husband Andrew, five cats, and a Great Dane.

Sophia Smyth—Leta's younger sister is married to Jeremy and lives in New Orleans.

Dave Prentiss—A journalist from NYC, he and Leta met when he stayed at the Olde Mill Inn in Astonbury. Nicknamed Tommy.

The Brits

Gemma Taylor—A Detective Inspector at the Stow-on-the-Wold police station, she's the daughter of Libby and Gavin and lives in the guest cottage behind the inn.

Wendy Davies—The retired English teacher from North Carolina returned to Astonbury to look after her mum and has become good friends with Leta.

Peter Davies—Wendy's twin and owner of the local garage, Peter is a cyclist and cricketer.

Belle Davies—Mother to Wendy and Peter, Belle lives at Sunshine Cottage with Wendy.

Rhiannon Smith—Rhiannon owns the Let It Be yoga studio where Leta and Wendy take classes.

Ellie, the Dowager Countess of Stow—Ellie lives in Astonbury Manor and is active in village affairs.

Matthew and Sarah Coates—Ellie's son and daughter-in-law, the Earl and Countess of Stow, live in a large cottage near the manor house.

Lucy Miller—A photographer and portrait artist, she is living in one of the artisan cottages on Astonbury Estate.

Mindy—Owner of Posh Pets.

Polly—Mindy's daughter, who works as a groomer at Posh Pets, also volunteers at Pepper's Animal Shelter.

Ric—A new groomer at Posh Pets, Ric also volunteers at Pepper's Animal Shelter most evenings.

Beatrix Scott—The owner of the Book Nook hosts monthly book club meetings.

Trixie Maxwell—Beatrix's niece works in the bookshop.

The Animals

Dickens—Leta's happy-go-lucky dwarf Great Pyrenees who loves belly rubs and everyone he meets.

Christie—The sassy, opinionated, and uppity black cat who rules the roost at Leta's Schoolhouse Cottage.

Paddington—The Burmese cat at the Olde Mill Inn, often terrorized by Christie.

Watson—The tabby who briefly lived at the inn but decided he preferred the manor house.

Blanche—Ellie's corgi enjoys romping with Dickens in the manor house when he and Leta visit.

Basil—The Great Pyrenees who protects the sheep on the estate and is fond of Dickens, calls Dickens Lil' Bit.

Buttercup—Lucy's part basset hound/part golden retriever becomes friends with Dickens.

Snowball—Rhiannon adopted the white kitten from the litter found in the donkey barn.

Spot—When Timmy's parents let him choose a kitten, he picked the calico and promptly named her Spot.

CHAPTER ONE

TURNING AND WAVING ONE last time, Dave walked into the Moreton-on-Marsh train station. "Love you, Tuppence. Thanksgiving will be here before you know it."

It had been a roller coaster month since his arrival in late September, and we were both taking this parting harder than usual. Starting with my concussion and culminating with a murder in Torquay, the events had combined to bring home how precious life was and how quickly it could change.

As I fastened my seatbelt, Christie piped up from the back seat. "Are we going to yoga now?"

I looked at my sleek black cat in the rearview mirror. Her head was peeking from the backpack, which was securely fastened to the seatbelt. "Yes, princess. We're headed that way. Will you be showing Snowball the ropes again today?"

If anyone noticed me talking when no one else was in the car, they'd either assume I was on my phone or I was crazy. Or they might think I was talking to my cat the way other people spoke to their four-legged companions. No one knew that I conversed with my pets and that we understood each other. I'd had this ability since I was a child and had quickly learned I was unique. Until and unless I found someone else with my talent, it would remain a secret between me and my furry friends.

Christie meowed, "Snowball is learning, but she's mostly a fluffy furball." Typical Christie comment. Snowball couldn't possibly be as good a yogi as she was.

Before I cranked my London taxi, I looked at the envelope Dave had left propped on the dashboard. He'd made me promise to open it only after I got home from yoga. Written on the front was the line from *Romeo and Juliet*, "Parting is such sweet sorrow." *That's what comes of dating a writer.* Dave was always ready with an appropriate quote.

Eyes focused on the road, my thoughts moved between Thanksgiving in Atlanta with Dave and my sisters and the happenings of the past month. Dave would soon be winging his way to New York City, and I needed to resolve the situation with my friend Peter. It was looking more and more as though I would have to take the bull by the horns. I refused to let myself believe that the awkwardness between us was permanent.

Enough. Go to yoga and enjoy yourself. I cranked up the radio and sang along to the Beatles station. Christie squeaked in protest, and I pictured her tucked in the backpack with her paws over her ears. I loved music, but I couldn't sing. Plenty would say I couldn't dance either.

Upstairs in Rhiannon's yoga studio, I greeted Wendy, lifted Christie from the backpack, and laid my mat next to my friend's. "Goodness, it's been ages since I've been to yoga, and I'm sure I'm going to pay for being such a slacker."

Wendy sat with the soles of her feet together and her knees falling out to the side. I never could quite get my knees to the floor in that pose, but she made it look easy. "Well, you *did* have a concussion, which put you out of commission for a bit."

"True. I plan to make three classes this week to make up for it."

As we chatted, Christie and Snowball darted around the studio. I looked toward the door when

I heard Rhiannon say, "Good morning, Lucy. I'm glad you could make it."

The newcomer grabbed two blankets and a yoga block and set up on the other side of Wendy. "Hello, ladies. I'm Lucy Miller."

Her short, curly, salt-and-pepper hair made me think she was in her fifties like Wendy and me. As we introduced ourselves, she noted my American accent. "Aha, you must be Dickens's and Christie's owner. Sarah said I should be sure to give you one of my cards."

My quizzical look must have caught her attention. "I'm a photographer and portrait artist, and I specialize in four-legged subjects." She explained she was an old friend of Sarah Coates, a.k.a. Lady Stow, and was staying in one of the artisan cottages that dotted the Astonbury Estate.

I still had a difficult time thinking of down-to-earth Sarah and her husband as the Countess and Earl of Stow. Matthew managed the estate, including the brewery and the sheep, and Sarah was renowned for the sheep's milk soap and lotions she produced. The cottages were filled with weavers, knitters, woodworkers, and potters, who, like Sarah, sold their wares at festivals and in shops across the Cotswolds.

"Pet portraits! That would make the perfect Christmas gift for Dave." I paused. "Are you already completely booked with holiday requests?"

"I have room for four additional commissions, but I need to schedule the photo sessions for this coming week. After that, I can't guarantee anything until the New Year. Shall we chat after class? I've got my photo book and my calendar in the car."

Wendy suggested Lucy join us for our usual post-yoga jaunt to Toby's Tearoom, where we could discuss the details. As Rhiannon hushed us and introduced her cat yogis Christie and Snowball, I thought of other villagers who might want to engage Lucy. Given that Lucy was staying on the estate, I wondered whether Ellie had already signed her up for a portrait of Blanche, her cute corgi.

It wasn't long before all thoughts of pet portraits disappeared from my brain as I focused on holding the yoga poses Rhiannon took us through. *Why does this class have to be standing poses?*

When we moved into corpse pose, Snowball chose my stomach as her perch. That was fine by me, as she was still a kitten and much lighter than Christie, who was nestled by Lucy's side. I gently lifted the white puffball as we shifted to cross-legged pose and said Namaste.

My legs felt weak as we made our way downstairs to the front door. "Oh my goodness, I'm already sore, and it's bound to be worse by tomorrow. I wonder if I can bribe Rhiannon to make Monday's class a restorative one."

"Leta, that's three days away. You've got all weekend to recover," Wendy chided me.

"Not if my plan works out. I'm determined to get your brother to cycle with me Sunday like we used to do. I only hope my legs are working by then."

Wendy rolled her eyes. "Well, good luck with that. I know how stubborn he's being about this."

We tossed our mats in our cars, and Lucy grabbed her portfolio. As we approached Toby's, I exclaimed over the fall colors displayed in the outdoor containers. "It looks like Jenny's outdone herself again. The mums with pumpkins and bundles of corn are perfect." Jenny was one of Toby's baristas and his go-to for decorating the shop.

Toby was manning the counter. "Ladies, welcome. Did Rhiannon wear you out this morning?"

As I groaned yes, Wendy introduced Lucy. We placed our orders for coffee, and I eyed the pumpkin scones. "Oh heck, Toby, let me have a scone too. But that's the last one until I leave for Atlanta. If I don't lose a few pounds before then, it will be a downhill slide until after Christmas."

Wendy and I had one of our typical conversations about how we'd be watching our weight until they carried us out the door feet first. We were both short, though at five feet, two inches, I was tall compared to Wendy at five feet nothing. I pictured her in the Peter Pan costume she'd worn again this year for the Fall Fête and could see her taking flight like Sandy Duncan or Mary Martin on Broadway. The mental image prompted me to describe our costumes to Lucy.

She placed her portfolio on the table. "Now, that would have made for some good photos. Sorry I missed it."

"Look, Wendy, she's already shot photos of Watson and Blanche." Watson, a handsome tabby, was the latest addition to Astonbury Manor, and he often visited Christie at my Schoolhouse Cottage.

Wendy pointed. "And look at the shots of Basil with the sheep. Are you painting all of these, Lucy? Or will some remain only as photographs?"

Our new friend laughed. "I can't help myself. Have camera, will travel—and shoot photos. No portraits of Basil, but Sarah may use a Basil shot in her booth at the tree lighting in December. With appropriate permissions, some of my photos also wind up in magazines and exhibits."

Christie meowed from her backpack, "Where are the cats?"

As if she understood, Lucy laughed. "Yes, Christie, there are cats. They're near the back of the book."

That prompted me to flip to the back, where there were plenty of cats plus a few cat and dog duos. "See, Christie, you and Dickens will be in good company."

I continued flipping through the album until an unusual dog caught my eye. "Oh my goodness! Is this not the cutest thing?"

Lucy smiled. "She's mine, or she is now. She was my sister's, but when she passed away, Buttercup came to me. I call her a *cuteapotamus*."

Looking from the photo to Lucy, Wendy asked, "And what exactly is she? She looks like a golden retriever, except her legs are short."

"Tanya got her from a farmer who said his basset hound fell in love with a golden, and Buttercup was the result, so she has the stature of a basset. She's a sweetheart."

Wendy and I continued to ooh and aah over the photos and portraits, and I began to envision a photoshoot at my cottage. Lucy penciled me in for Tuesday afternoon and asked if I had a preference as to indoors or outdoors. In my head, I saw my four-legged friends posed in front of the fireplace, so we agreed indoors would be best. Lucy said she'd look over the house and make recommendations for possible spots.

The envelope on the dashboard beckoned to me on the drive home, so I grabbed it as soon as I parked in my driveway. Smiling again at the quote from *Romeo and Juliet*, I opened the flap to see one of Trixie's handcrafted cards—a design I hadn't seen before. It was an old-fashioned inkwell with a red feathered quill, much like the gift Dave had gotten me from The Quill bookshop in Torquay. Smiling, I touched the tiny feather. *I bet he asked her to make this especially for me.* Inside, Trixie had calligraphed the quote, "The most beautiful part is, I wasn't even looking when I found you!" This sentiment dovetailed with the playful debate we'd had over the past week as to who found whom and who was luckier.

After my husband died, I never imagined I'd find love again. As the card said, I wasn't even looking. I let Christie in the house and Dickens out before

I walked to the stone marker in the backyard. Ellie had given it to me on the second anniversary of Henry's death in Atlanta, saying she wanted me to have a small remembrance here. Kneeling, I touched the bronze plaque affixed to the stone. What would Henry think of the new man in my life? *He's happy for me. I just know it.*

Dickens snuffled around the stone wall and unearthed a ball in one corner. After throwing it a few times, we moved inside, where I built a fire. I placed Dave's card on the mantel and settled on the couch with my tablet. Dave had sent me two emails, one with a link to an article in the *Strand Magazine* and another telling me he missed me already.

I pictured him writing in his New York City apartment, visiting his gym, and taking long walks in Central Park. Was it only a month ago that he'd suggested leaving it behind to move to England—to be with me? *I think I'm the lucky one.*

Astonbury was my home now. When I was house-hunting in the Cotswolds, I stayed at the Olde Mill Inn, and that's where I met Peter and Wendy. Libby and Gavin, the owners, often invited local friends to meet their guests over cocktails on Friday evenings. It was Peter who convinced me to purchase a refurbished London taxi. He was also the person who pushed me to get back on my bicycle, something I'd avoided after Henry's death in a cycling accident.

It was time for me to tackle Peter. I kept thinking the tension between us would dissipate, but it had been nearly six weeks, and nothing had changed. True, my concussion had put a temporary halt to our Sunday bicycle rides, and Dave's visit meant I wasn't as available as I usually was, but I knew none of that was the problem. When I asked Peter to cycle the weekend Dave was in Carlisle for a literary festival, he brushed me off with a terse text—something he'd never done before.

So much has happened this last month. Dave had arrived just in time to take care of me after I sustained an injury in one of my unfortunate sleuthing activities, as my sister Sophia referred to them. Peter found me unconscious at the donkey barn and called A&E, but it was Dave who played nurse as I recovered. He walked Dickens, cooked, and ensured that I followed all the doctor's orders.

It was also Dave who first noticed a change in Peter's behavior. He thought the huge flower arrangement from him, plus what Dave described as Peter's seeming possessiveness when he brought me home from the hospital, signaled a shift in his feelings for me.

I told myself Dave was mistaken and was overreacting but wondered whether I had willed myself to overlook the signals. I saw the two of us as pals and wanted to believe Peter did too.

Fortunately, during my recovery, Peter checked on my health via Dave and Wendy instead of directly with me. That seemed odd, but it allowed me to delay dealing with the situation. Given Dave's tender ministrations and his swoon-worthy declaration that he wanted to leave New York City to be with me, I had managed to push thoughts of Peter to the back of my mind for weeks. Still, I couldn't ignore his absence. Dave and Peter had developed a camaraderie since they'd met a year ago, and the three of us often shared pints at the pub when Dave visited, but not on this trip.

Now, with Dave on his way to New York City, I no longer had any excuse to avoid dealing with it. Before my concussion, we'd cycled every Sunday for months, only skipping a day when I traveled. Well, we also skipped a day when I nearly drowned in the River Elfe, but that was another story.

I texted him that I was ready to get back in the saddle and that I wanted to cycle on Sunday. For the second time, he put me off with a text: "Not sure. Swamped at the garage."

He's not going to make this easy. Next, I left a voicemail. "Peter, we need to talk, whether it's during a bike ride or over coffee. You decide." The ball was back in his court.

It was hours before he responded, hours where I vacillated between irritation and worry. Finally, his text came in. "Fine. Cycle to Stow and have breakfast." With that settled, all I had to do was figure out what to say. Should I discuss it with Wendy? She was, after all, my best friend in Astonbury, but she was also Peter's twin sister.

I thought back to her reaction when she saw the floral arrangement on my dining room table. She assumed they were from Dave and seemed shocked or puzzled or something when I told her they were from Peter. I too thought they were from Dave until I read the card. I quickly—perhaps too quickly—took the gesture as a heartfelt thank you for the work the Little Old Ladies' Detective agency did for him. When he hired us to solve the mystery of his friend's death, we did exactly that. *Isn't it natural to send a thank you for a job well done?*

Never one to shy away from a confrontation, she gave her brother a hard time about the flowers the very next day and told me he'd turned beet red and made noises about it being a simple thank you for the Little Old Ladies solving his friend's murder. Except, as Wendy had pointed out, she and Belle didn't get any flowers, and they were members of the LOLs.

There was nothing for it but to call Wendy. "Can you come over? I need your help."

"Sure. Do I get a hint, or do I have to wait until I get there? And is there wine involved?"

"No hints, but yes, there will be wine, and possibly cheese and crackers. Who knows, if you play your cards right, I might even feed you a Greek salad for dinner." That sealed the deal.

Dickens greeted her in his usual boisterous style, running to the car when she pulled up and barking hello. As soon as they came inside, he rolled over. "Can I have a belly rub, please?"

All Wendy heard was a bark, but she got the message. Handing me a bottle of wine, she knelt and cooed, "You handsome boy. You want a belly rub?"

Christie strutted in and rubbed against her legs before turning to me. "Where's my food?" She was a demanding thing and had me well trained. I placed a forkful of wet food in her dish and watched.

She sniffed it and stood back. "Fluff it, Leta. What's wrong with you?" That meant I had to move the dollop to the center of the dish and stir it until she was satisfied. When she was happy, I turned my attention to pouring two glasses of wine.

With a plate of brie and crackers, we took our wine glasses and moved to the sitting room. Dickens and Christie followed, and we all settled in front of the fireplace.

"Okay, Leta, what do you need my help with?"

"Your brother. After a month of avoiding me, he's agreed to a bicycle outing on Sunday. Now I need to figure out what to say to him."

That got a chuckle. "You know he's not going to want to talk about any of this, right? He still maintains you deserved the flowers because you were the only LOL who was injured, though I'm not buying it."

"Are you saying you agree with Dave? That it was a what—a romantic gesture?"

She rolled her eyes. "You can be so naïve. Look, it's obvious to me that his feelings went from friendly to romantic, if only briefly. He was in a fragile emotional state on the heels of Rupert's death, and he was already experiencing a 'life can change in a heartbeat' moment. When he found you unconscious, he worked himself into a state. That's my take."

"Do you think by now he's realized that it was an aberration?"

"Pfft. You're giving him more credit than he's due. Think about it. He's a confirmed bachelor in his fifties. We know of only one girlfriend, and that didn't last long. Do you honestly think he's analyzed his emotions? Nope. He's regretting the flowers, and he's embarrassed—possibly even worried that he's jeopardized your friendship. But he's a man, and he doesn't know what to do about it. I mean, have you ever known a man to utter the words, 'we need to talk'? I sure haven't."

That was all I needed to hear, and I knew just how to broach the subject with him.

On Sunday, I did my usual groaning about the cool damp weather as we set off from Peter's garage. He was quiet, but now that I thought I knew what was up, I took it in stride. In Stow, we parked our bicycles in front of Huffkin's and shed our jackets as we found a table.

Once we had our coffee, I dove in. "Peter, I haven't seen hide nor hair of you since you brought me home from A&E, and that's odd. I know it took me a few days to send a proper thank-you note for the flowers, but I can't imagine you being put out over that. What's going on? Have I done something to upset you?"

He ducked his head and sighed but was spared from answering when the waitress came to take our orders. When she left us, he picked up with, "Chilly ride today, wasn't it?"

I'm not letting him off the hook that easily. "Peter, is it that I missed the Celebration of Life for Rupert? Is that it?"

Running his hand through his hair, he finally answered me. "No, Leta. You had a concussion, for goodness' sake. I didn't expect you to come. Don't be daft."

He stared at his mug of coffee, as though the answer might be lurking there. "Look, I don't know how to say this. Rupert dying in the prime of his life, you helping me deal with it . . . finding you unconscious . . . it was all too much. Bloody hell, I even thought about you losing Henry, and then I thought, 'What would I do if you didn't make it?' I worked myself into a lather."

I wanted to reach out and tell him it was okay, not to worry about it, but if there was any hope we were going to get through this, I needed to hear him out.

"Aaargh. You and me . . . we're mates. I mean, I hit the pub with the blokes from the cricket team, but I've never had a woman as a friend—someone to cycle with and meet for dinner and a pint. You know I'm a quiet sort, but you manage to get me talking, and I enjoy it. I like hanging out with you and Wendy, *and* with you and Dave."

"But?"

"But as soon as Wendy asked me where the flowers were for her and Mum, I knew I'd messed up, and I've been embarrassed about it ever since." He shook his head, muttering, "Those bloody flowers. Listen, I'm happy for you. I'm happy Dave is moving to Astonbury. I just want you to know, that if you need me, I'm here."

The corners of my mouth tilted up. "Like the song?"

"Huh?"

"The song, 'You've Got a Friend.' I can hear Carole King singing it. You know, I've only had one other close male friend. We were in college together, and I always knew he was there for me. Even after he moved across the country, I saw him whenever he made it back to Atlanta." I squinted. "So, we're good?"

"Yes, Leta, we are." *Thank goodness.*

We sipped our coffees, and Peter caught me up on village happenings. When I mentioned the photoshoot for Dickens and Christie, he grinned. "I knew you'd sign up once you met Lucy. Did you know she spent almost an entire day at the donkey barn? Martha and Dylan may soon be famous."

Regular walks with Dickens to feed the donkeys were part of my routine. "Ooh, I'd love to get one of her photos to include with a column. My editors in the States would adore that." I wrote a column for two small papers in Georgia and North Carolina, and my readers were enchanted with my move to England.

As our waitress set our plates down, I continued. "So, you've met Lucy?"

"Yes. Sarah sent her to me to fix that ancient Land Rover she drives. She seems to be settling in, but how long she'll be here is up in the air—at least through the holidays, I think." He explained she'd given up her flat in London to move in with her sister in Kingham. "When Tanya was diagnosed with terminal cancer, Lucy cared for her but was at loose ends after she died. I gather she used to travel a good bit, so when Sarah offered to let her stay in a cottage on the estate, she jumped at the chance. She and Sarah were at university together."

"The holidays can be so hard. It will be good for her to be busy with portraits and to have the company of Sarah and the others on the estate. Have you met that adorable dog?"

"Oh, yes. They're like you and Dickens. Buttercup was always at her sister's side, and now she's attached to Lucy. That's part of what Lucy needs to sort—what to do with Buttercup when she starts traveling again."

As we paid our bill and returned to our bicycles, I thought about Lucy. *Maybe she'll decide to stay.*

CHAPTER TWO

ON MONDAY, DICKENS AND I paid a visit to Posh
Pets so he would look his best for the Tuesday
photoshoot with Lucy. Though he always balked
when we arrived, he never failed to be cheerful
when I picked him up. Mindy, the owner, said his
attitude shifted once the bath part was over. As
I took the leash from her freckle-faced daughter
Polly, I dropped my usual £20 donation into the
box for Pepper's Animal Shelter.

"Are you still volunteering at the shelter, Polly?"

"Yes, Mrs. Parker, every Tuesday after work. I'd adopt them all if I could." She knelt to give Dickens a hug.

When Lucy arrived the next day, I let Dickens out to greet her. "Look, Leta, her dog is my size."

As the two did their introductory sniffing, Lucy and I marveled at their almost identical stature. Buttercup was longer than Dickens, but with their short legs, their shoulders were the same height. She had long golden hair compared to Dickens's wavy white coat, and her snout was slightly more pointed.

What an adorable duo. "How cute! They look like the perfect couple. Does Buttercup like to chase balls?"

"Yes, but not as much as she did when she was younger. Did you notice her head tilt? She had a bout of vestibular disease a year ago, and she's not as frisky as she once was. They call it old dog disease, you know."

Kneeling, I stroked Buttercup's shiny coat. "Yes, Dickens's predecessor had it, and his head tilt never went away. Banjo always looked as though he had a question, and his balance stayed a bit off. How old is Buttercup?"

"She's ten and, of course, has no idea there's anything amiss. Poor thing, she's also blind in one eye, which is probably why chasing balls is a challenge. But she's a trooper."

Dickens dropped a ball at Buttercup's feet. "Leta, I can bring her balls. She doesn't have to chase them."

I smiled at my boy. "Looks as though Dickens wants to take care of her. I hope you'll take some photos of the two of them. This has the makings of a column." I told her about my "Parker's Pen" column and my idea to use one of her donkey photos too. "I often post my tales on the *Astonbury*

Aha, and the villagers are sure to get a kick out of both topics. I find that everyone loves animals."

We carried her equipment inside to the kitchen, where Christie greeted us in her typical sassy fashion. "I hear you're going to take my picture, though I don't know why Dickens has to be involved."

As she twined herself around Lucy's ankles, I explained how I had acquired both Christie and Dickens in Atlanta. "My husband and I fell in love with Dickens the first time we saw a photo of him online, but it was Dickens who chose Christie, or maybe vice versa. She was part of a litter at the horse farm on our road. When he moved in to sniff her where she was nestled in a bale of hay, she latched her tiny paws onto his nose and wouldn't let go. I was leaning towards the calico kitten, but Dickens wanted Christie."

Christie meowed, "Why you would want a blotchy cat is beyond me."

Lucy wanted to see all the rooms in the cottage for ideas on where to pose my four-legged companions. "Goodness. It would be difficult for me to travel if I had a place like this. I'd never want to leave."

"I must admit I love my cottage. It's everything I want it to be—cozy yet roomy, with all my favorite colors."

"Let's set up in the sitting room with the fireplace, but I also want to see if we can get Christie to pose in front of the bookcase in your office, maybe even on one of the shelves. The white woodwork with the red walls would be a perfect backdrop."

We spent several hours moving my furry friends around, while Buttercup snoozed on Dickens's dog bed near the fire. It was as though Lucy had trained her to stay out of the way.

"Dickens and Christie may be the best models I've had. If I didn't know better, I'd think they understood what we're trying to do."

Christie meowed from her perch on the bookshelf. "Silly girl. Of course I understand. Now, are you getting my best side?"

It was going to be difficult for me to pick which photo would make the best portrait, but Lucy promised to make suggestions and possibly combine bits from several shots into a final product.

We looked through the shots over a pot of tea at the kitchen table. "Leta, this one in front of the fireplace with Christie leaning her head into Dickens's neck is adorable, but I like the bookcase better as the background. I may shift that around to make it work."

Christie joined us in the kitchen, but Dickens was curled up with Buttercup on the dog bed. We had to wake them when Lucy was ready to leave. I helped her load the car, and we laughed at the two dogs roaming my garden. Like Dickens, Buttercup was especially interested in sniffing the stone wall that surrounded it.

"Let's go, Buttercup." The *cuteapotamus* climbed into the car with some help as Dickens watched.

"Lucy, what do you think about me bringing Dickens over for a play date with Buttercup? Would you be okay with her wandering the estate with him? It's like one big dog park."

"Believe it or not, I was thinking the same thing. She can't keep up with Basil, but I think Dickens would wait for her, don't you? I like to take her with me, but not all my subjects are as receptive as your two." We agreed the two dogs were destined to be good friends and set a date for the next afternoon. I would arrive with Dickens and a book in time for Lucy to leave for an appointment in Stow. The dogs could roam while I put my feet up to read.

I emailed Dave a photo of Buttercup and Dickens and explained she was a precious mix of basset hound and golden retriever. "Dickens has the same short legs since he's a dwarf Great Pyrenees, and they make a perfect pair."

The rest of the afternoon I spent ensconced on the couch in front of the fire with a new book. My sister Anna had recommended *The Dog Who Rescues Cats*, a true story about a dog who had a knack for finding feral cats.

As I read a few passages aloud to Dickens, he barked his amazement. "Ginny found cats in old buildings? Like we found the kittens in the donkey barn?"

Laughing at his enthusiasm, I had to convince him that we did *not* need to start searching for cats. "Dickens, plenty of people take stray cats and dogs to animal shelters so they can find good homes. We have enough to keep us busy without getting involved in rescuing lost animals."

I imagined myself telling the members of the Little Old Ladies' Detective agency that we had a new mission. Instead of solving murder cases, we could track lost pets—much less dangerous, for sure. *Nah, not going to happen.*

The month of November flew by, and before I knew it, I was on my way to Atlanta for Thanksgiving. My next-door neighbors the Watsons would take care of Christie, and little Timmy was excited about bringing Spot to visit. The name he'd given his calico kitten made me laugh whenever I thought of it.

Peter planned to stop by to walk Dickens as usual, but at the last minute, Lucy offered to take care of him. It was a short walk from Astonbury Estate to my cottage, and she thought Buttercup would enjoy a twice-daily outing. When she asked if I'd be okay with Dickens staying with them on the estate part of the time, I readily agreed. He was an outgoing, happy-go-lucky boy and adored

Basil and Blanche both. Now, he'd have three friends to visit—a Great Pyrenees, a corgi, and a *cuteapotamus*.

Thanksgiving was a whirlwind of friends, family, and food. Anna outdid herself with dessert offerings—poundcake, pecan pie, brownies, and carrot cake. In addition to turkey and dressing, we enjoyed a leg of lamb, pastitsio, and an assortment of Greek pastries. With our Greek heritage and Southern upbringing, there was never a shortage of good food.

Dave flew down for the feast, and then we jetted off to NYC early Friday to view the Christmas lights and windows and visit his mother and sister in Connecticut. It boded well that both our families were happy about his upcoming move to England.

In less than a month, Dave would join me in Astonbury for Christmas, and by late January he'd be here to stay. I could hardly wait.

CHAPTER THREE

IT TOOK ME MOST of Monday to recover from my overseas jaunt, but by Tuesday morning, I was ready to dive into the week's activities, starting with yoga. From there I grabbed a coffee at Toby's and crossed the street to the Book Nook to help Trixie fill small drawstring bags with bookmarks and magnets to give out on Friday night. The popular village bookshop would have a booth at the annual tree lighting on the village green and would draw a crowd of villagers eager to purchase holiday books and stationery as gifts.

Tommy and Tuppence were lounging in the front window beneath the Christmas tree and meowed lazily as I entered. Neither could be bothered to leave their comfortable perch, but Trixie greeted me with a cheery, "Welcome home, Leta. How was the trip?"

I pulled out my phone to show her the Macy's windows decked in their Christmas finery. She was enchanted with them as well as the holiday booths set up at Bryant Park.

"Did you come back laden with purchases, or did you resist temptation?"

Shaking my head, I confessed I'd been unable to resist a new satin dress for the Saturday night party at the manor house, but assured her that I planned to do most of my Christmas shopping at the tree lighting. "I'll be standing in line for Sarah's sheep's milk lotion and soaps. And I hear the new weaver on the estate has some lovely place mats and runners. I'm sure I need a set for my holiday dinner."

We made short work of filling the bags, and I stopped by the front desk to chat with Beatrix. "The window looks lovely with the tree and the elves. And, of course, your librarian scarecrow is quite festive."

"I found those red reading glasses and the plaid shawl in a thrift shop and knew I had to have them. She's held up amazingly well, much like Raggedy Ann and Andy at the inn. They're in their candy cane outfits again this year." Scarecrows were auctioned off at the Fall Fête each year to raise money for local charities, and Libby and Beatrix had gotten theirs a year ago. They had great fun outfitting them for the different seasons.

Saying I'd see her Friday, I set off to walk the mile to my cottage. It was time to drag out my boxes of decorations in preparation for picking out my trees come the weekend. As he did last year, Peter would take Belle, Wendy, and me to Broadway to pick out trees and wreaths on Saturday. I would get a small tree for my office and decorate it with cat ornaments. The larger tree would go in the sitting room. Christmas was my favorite season, and if I had my way, Christmas lights would stay up until at least February.

Done and dusted. I washed my hands after transferring the boxes from the garage to my office, and then plopped on the couch. Pulling a throw across my legs, I checked my email. I saw a note from Libby, which was unusual, as the phone was her preferred mode of communication. She had forwarded me something about a lost dog, and when I opened it, I knew why. Our local constable's dog had been missing since Sunday—well, more accurately, his sister's dog.

We were all fond of Constable Jonas James, and I hoped the family pet would soon be found. Much as I did with Dickens, his sister often let the dog play in the garden bordered by stone walls, but never allowed it to stay outdoors overnight. Libby mentioned that maybe I'd catch sight of it on one of my many walks. When I checked the news on the *Astonbury Aha*, I saw that Jonas had posted a notice there too. What was interesting was that there was also another missing dog listed.

Dickens was stretched out in front of the fire but stirred when I nudged him with my foot. "Dickens, how about a walk to see the donkeys?"

He perked right up. "Yes, yes, the donkeys."

It was a bit chilly for Christie to join us in her backpack, so we left her behind. I bundled up in my jacket, gloves, and fleece headband and grabbed carrots for the donkeys. Martha and Dylan were especially fond of carrots.

I explained to Dickens on the way that two dogs were missing, and we needed to keep an eye out. "I know you're not a bloodhound, but perhaps you'll catch their scent. Jonas and the other owner must be frantic. I can't imagine how I'd feel if you or Christie went missing."

He barked over his shoulder. "I'm not going anywhere, Leta."

Martha and Dylan trotted towards us as Dickens barked a greeting. Those two were one of the many things I loved about my new home. They chomped on carrots as I stroked their warm noses and Dickens stood on his hind legs. One by one, the donkeys lowered their heads to nudge him.

"Dickens, shall we go on to the inn? We've got several hours before the sun sets." Of course, he was agreeable. He'd probably missed seeing Paddington while I was gone. Libby and Gavin's Burmese cat liked to romp with Dickens, and one of their favorite pastimes was diving in the dirty linens that Jill collected when she stripped the beds in the guest rooms. Dickens got on with

Paddington much better than Christie did. *Because he's loveable, and the princess is uppity.*

The scarecrows were dressed in their striped mittens and scarves, and Paddington was lolling on the pathway in front of them. When I opened the front door, he and Dickens darted inside. "Libby, Gavin, it's Leta."

Walking past the conservatory door, I saw Gavin at his desk. "Hi. Back from your travels, I see. Libby's in the kitchen."

Libby was stirring a pot of something that smelled wonderful. "It's my mum's recipe for London Particular. Here's a spoon. Give it a try."

"Yum. Like split pea soup, but different. You'll have to give me the recipe, but first, tell me about the name."

"A London Particular is what we call a thick London smog. In the days of gas street lamps, it took on a yellow tinge. If I recall correctly, Charles Dickens mentions it in *Bleak House*. You know, fog, thick as pea soup? Except we usually use yellow split peas, not green."

"Not a very appetizing name, is it? I've always liked pea soup but gave up making it because Henry didn't care for it. I wonder whether Dave would like it."

That comment led to a conversation about my trip home and Dave's imminent move before Libby shifted to village news. "Jill's going to stay here Friday night so Gavin and I can both see the tree lighting. I don't feel right leaving our guests on their own, so it was nice of her to offer. Goodness, it will be almost like a date." Last year, Libby had stayed behind while Gavin attended and helped Matthew with the kegs of Astonbury Ale. I anticipated he'd have a keg of his new Cycling Cider available too.

I laughed. "Well, Dickens will be my date, and he's sure to get lots of belly rubs while we're there.

That reminds me, what's the story about Jonas's dog? Has it ever gone missing before?"

Libby grimaced. "It's his sister's dog, but no. It has a doghouse in the garden, and Jonas's sister often lets it stay outside during the day. This has never happened before. Jonas thinks someone took it."

"Why would he think that? Couldn't it have wandered off?"

"He says the little thing is too short to get over the wall, and he's sure his sister wouldn't leave the gate open, though there's a chance his little niece might have."

"Either way, it's terrible to lose a pet. I leave Dickens in the garden all the time—not when I leave the house, but when I'm doing things inside and he's enjoying himself out there. I'll have to be more careful."

I made a copy of the soup recipe and returned home with Dickens. The sun would soon set, and the wind had picked up, which pleased him no end. The breeze ruffled his thick white coat as he pranced along, jabbering about this and that—Paddington, donkeys, and the chill in the air.

The next day Christie was still shunning me, as she'd been doing since I returned from my trip. Of course, she didn't shun the food I provided, but she *did* manage to be even haughtier than usual as she meowed her criticism about how it looked in the dish. When she deemed it edible, she ate it and then disappeared.

This morning when I took my coffee to the office, she deigned to join me. First, she demanded treats, and then she gave me an earful about my absence. "I can't believe you left me here without Dickens. He's not much company, but he's better than Timmy! And where was Peter? I like Peter. He rubs my head, and he knows how I like my food." She continued in that vein for a few minutes before running out of steam and curling up in the file drawer. I wondered whom she missed more—me, Dickens, or Peter. *Who am I kidding? I know it was Peter.*

After answering a few emails, I wrote a column about Thanksgiving weekend in New York City, a topic I knew my readers would adore. Next was a trip to the market for the ingredients for a big pot of vegetable soup and a pan of cornbread, perfect for the cold, damp Cotswolds weather. I had sent Lucy a Jacquie Lawson e-card Monday thanking her for taking care of Dickens and inviting her and Buttercup for dinner, and I was looking forward to seeing her that evening.

I knew Christie hadn't completely thawed when she failed to join me in the kitchen while I cooked. Dickens, on the other hand, was his usual chipper self, and he was excited that Buttercup was coming over. He had regaled me nonstop with tales of their adventures on the estate, and it was clear the two dogs had become boon companions.

As I set the table, Dickens lay by the kitchen door. "Buttercup likes the sheep, but we stayed closer to the sheep barn than Basil does. And Watson? She likes Watson. We followed him to the river and watched him cross over. Buttercup stuck her front paws in, but I told her Lucy wouldn't be happy if she got muddy." I'd forgotten the Watson story of how he took a shortcut across the river by traversing the tree limbs that joined from either side. And Dickens was right to caution Buttercup. My boy might have been able to cross in a shallow spot, but the current could have proven too strong for the older dog.

"You're a good friend, Dickens. Did you play ball, too?"

"Not much. Buttercup likes to carry the ball around, but she's not big on chasing it. I left my red ball there for her."

When our guests arrived, I gave the dogs treats and poured wine for Lucy and me. Lucy had lots of stories about the dogs exploring the estate. "It's funny. I think Dickens has given Buttercup a new lease on life. I think dogs can be melancholy, don't you?"

I remembered how Dickens had been after Henry died and agreed with her. "Does Buttercup still miss your sister?"

"That's my sense. Sometimes she's fine. Other times, she's subdued and seems to age before my eyes. There was none of that last week with Dickens around. They romped in the cottage and checked on the sheep. The times I went with them, I was astounded at how far they went. And let me tell you what she did the day I brought Dickens home!"

"By the way, it was good of you to do that. It was nice to open the door and see him Monday. So, what did Buttercup do?"

"The little stinker. I dropped Dickens off here on the way to Stow for a photoshoot, and I left Buttercup at home." She pointed at her dog. "Imagine my surprise when I came by your cottage on the way to the estate and saw this one lying in your driveway."

That was worrisome. Schoolhouse Lane wasn't a busy road, but there was some traffic. I was fortunate that Dickens knew better than to leave the driveway without me.

"You know, I leave for France tomorrow, and I'm a bit worried about Sarah looking after Buttercup, but she's assured me she won't let her out of her sight. Other than that spot of worry, I'm looking forward to the trip. I'm visiting a friend in Provence, and she's lined up several commissions for me with her neighbors. When I return next

Saturday, I'll have plenty of work to keep me busy through February at least."

When we moved to the kitchen for dinner, I brought out the thank you gift I'd brought back from Atlanta. "I hope Buttercup likes it."

Lucy unwrapped the small box and exclaimed over its contents. "Look, Buttercup, a new collar. And it has your name on it." I'd chosen a green plaid collar with an engraved brass name tag. Dickens had a new red one just like it, as did Christie.

Dickens barked. "Are we twins now?"

Unfastening Buttercup's old collar, Lucy attached the new one. "Now, that's adorable. She's all set for the holidays. Here, let me get a picture of the two of them." She tucked the old collar into her purse and pulled out her phone.

In a moment, my phone pinged with the photo, and I laughed as I showed it to Dickens. "Look, you're a photogenic pair."

Christie chose that moment to grace us with her presence and her opinion. "Oh, please, enough with the dogs. You know I'm the prettiest pet."

CHAPTER FOUR

THE TREE LIGHTING WAS the official kickoff to Astonbury's holiday season, and the villagers went all out for the event. Booths dotted the village green, and a huge tree stood in the center, waiting for the Earl of Stow to throw the switch. Many of the decorations were stored in the Village Hall, and new handmade ornaments were added every year by the village pre-schoolers. Their contributions ringed the lower branches of the tree—the ones they could reach. This year, the theme was candy canes.

As Dickens pranced in the cold evening air, I tugged my scarf over my nose. He barked and took off when he saw Basil with the sheep. He adored the large white dog, and the feeling seemed mutual. I heard Basil bark a greeting in response. "Hi, Lil' Bit." Dickens tolerated that nickname from Basil, but if anyone else referenced his diminutive stature, he barked in indignation.

I waved at George Evans and Rory Fox at the Cotswolds Tours booth and noted Rory's red fleece with the tour logo. A firm believer in the one for you, one for me holiday shopping method, I knew I'd have to get two of those—one for me and one for my sister Sophia.

My priority was a pint of Cycling Cider from Matthew's booth. Gavin was pouring, and Matthew's son Sam was straightening a stack of dark green fleece pullovers. He grinned as I approached. "Hi Leta. Don't you need a new pullover?" When he held it up, I saw the new Cycling Cider logo in gold stitching.

"Now, that's tempting, except I wish you had it in red. Maybe I'll get one for Dave." I looked around. "Gavin, where's Libby?"

He handed me a cup of cider and pointed. "Shopping, of course. I can see she's already stocked up on sheep's milk soap and is headed to the woolens."

Spotting Wendy and Peter approaching with Belle between them, I waved. She was so bundled up that I wouldn't have recognized her but for the white hair peeking from beneath her blue knitted cap. Pale blue was her color, just as red was mine.

Knowing Sarah had seasonal scents for soaps and lotions, I made a beeline for her booth. "I have plenty of your lavender lotion, but I'm here to stock up on the balsam selection—lotion, hand soap, and dishwashing liquid."

With her long brown hair in a braid down her back, she was the epitome of an earth mother. "It's going fast, so you better grab it while you can."

I pulled off my gloves and squirted a sample into one palm. "Oh my gosh. I need sets for each bathroom and one for the kitchen. Hopefully, I'll find balsam candles in Broadway tomorrow."

As she wrapped my purchases, I looked behind the table. "Did you bring Buttercup?"

She frowned. "I planned to, but she's been strange since Lucy left. I heard from our new woodworker that Buttercup's been making the rounds of the cottages each morning after I let her out. And Lucy told me she found her in your driveway this week, so I'm not taking any chances. Tonight, she's safely tucked away at our house."

Dickens had returned to my side. "Leta, hurry. Polly's at a booth, and she has treats!"

He turned and I followed. The Posh Pets booth was decorated with photos of shelter pets in festive bandannas, and a variety of holiday bandannas were for sale, with all proceeds going to Pepper's Animal Shelter. Polly and the tall, gangly young man by her side were doing a brisk business.

"Polly, what a great idea. As you can see, Dickens already has a red holiday collar, but here's a donation."

When I introduced myself to her partner, he replied, "Good to meet you. I'm Ric, and that's awfully generous of you. The shelter needs all the help it can get." He grinned at Dickens. "Polly's told me all about Dickens. I just started at Posh Pets, so maybe I'll get to see him again. And it looks as though he needs a treat."

I chuckled. "You have no idea. He always needs a treat."

At the booth of sweaters and scarves, I spied Libby holding up a navy-blue sweater for her daughter to inspect. Gemma pointed to a taupe and rust marled crewneck. "No, Mum, this would look better on Jake." Gemma was our local detective inspector, and her boyfriend, Jake, was a DI in Truro. The two had become an item after a murder investigation in August.

"I agree with you, Gemma. With Jake's coloring, rust is the way to go. Navy would be good for your dad, though."

Her blonde ponytail bounced as she nodded. "I should have asked you first, Leta. That settles it, and that's two Christmas gifts taken care of." She handed her credit card to the vendor and turned to survey the crowd. "Mum, can I get you to carry the bag, please? It wouldn't do for me to carry it around while I'm on duty."

We both looked up at the sound of a crackling microphone. Matthew Coates, the Earl of Stow, was standing by the tree, with several children by his feet.

"Greetings and Merry Christmas." He was attired in a plaid woolen waistcoat, a red velvet riding jacket, black riding breeches, and knee-high black leather boots. A black top hat completed the ensemble, and I knew from his mother, Ellie, that this was the outfit his father had worn in his role as the master of ceremonies.

"I am honored to be here tonight to light the Astonbury tree. My father started this tradition nearly forty years ago, and it was his favorite event of the season. I like to think he's looking down and smiling." He thanked the community for organizing the event and pointed toward the choir assembled in front of the village hall, asking for applause.

I wondered whether he had considered mentioning his nephew, Nicholas, who had stood in that spot last year. Tragically, his tenure as Earl had been cut short when he died in an auto accident, and the title had passed to Matthew. *It's probably better he didn't bring it up.*

Turning to a little girl who stood with her arms outstretched, he lifted her to his shoulder. In a green velvet dress and cape with a matching green bonnet tied beneath her chin, she looked like something from a Dickens novel.

Matthew smiled at her. "Are you ready?" She responded with a nervous giggle and pointed the remote control toward the tree. When she pressed the button, the tree sprang to life, and the villagers clapped. This was the cue for the choir to break into "Joy to the World."

I felt a touch on my elbow and turned to see Ellie. "He did a nice job, didn't he?"

"That he did. That little girl was a charming touch." I gave her a peck on the cheek. "Now, I need to find Dickens and head home. I need my beauty sleep if I'm going to look my best for your party tomorrow night."

It didn't take long to locate my boy. He was in the first spot I looked—the booth with holiday pictures drawn by the preschoolers. Surrounded by children giving him belly rubs, I knew he was in hog heaven. My boy was a fiend for belly rubs.

"Time to go home, young man." Leaping up, he shook himself and bounded to my side.

I called Dave as we strolled home. As I described the scene, I imagined him being here next Christmas. "Just think, the tree lighting, Ellie's party at the manor house—you have so much to look forward to."

He chuckled. "Yes, Tuppence, but most of all, I'm looking forward to being with you for every bit of it."

"You *do* say all the right things, Tommy."

On Saturday's tree shopping expedition, Wendy was bouncing with excitement, and I knew it wasn't about Christmas trees. Peter poked fun at her. "Wendy, I haven't seen you like this in ages. Is Rhys Ford that special?"

She stuck out her tongue. "Yes, he is. Not to mention, I have an honest-to-goodness date for a black-tie affair instead of my twin as an escort." She could joke, but I knew it was Rhys she was excited about. She had reconnected with her university friend at a literary conference in Torquay, and they were immediately drawn to each other. Initially, I'd had doubts about him, but he had proven me wrong in a memorable way.

Peter's truck was filled to the gills with trees, wreaths, and garland, and he'd carefully arranged it all so my purchases were on top. Belle stayed in the truck while we three unloaded two trees, a potted juniper, and three wreaths into the house. As Peter put the big tree in a stand in the sitting room, Wendy pulled me aside. "Can you come over in an hour or two? I need help choosing the right jewelry for my new dress." *She really is beside herself.*

"Let's say thirty minutes. That way I can squeeze in a nap and still have time to soak in the tub with my Shalimar bath oil. It's all part of the beauty ritual, you know."

Wendy greeted me at the door of Sunshine Cottage. "Shh, Mum's having her afternoon lie-down." Belle was the only other person I knew who took regular naps. My friends teased me about my nap habit, but I considered it one of the perks of retirement.

Sitting on the bed in Wendy's room, I watched as she pulled her new dress from the closet. The icy blue metallic knit was the perfect color for my platinum blonde friend, and the A-line cut with a V-neck showed off her petite frame. The dress shimmered as she pulled it over her head. When she added a simple necklace with a pear-shaped aquamarine stone, the look was complete.

"I think you've nailed it on the first try, Wendy. Add your tiny blue studs, and you'll be done."

"I was hoping you'd say that. I'm so nervous about seeing Rhys again, I can't think straight."

When I gave her a questioning look, she tried to explain. "I know we're attracted to each other, but I'm worried that this is too soon after Emily's death. What if I'm a temporary lifeline, and he doesn't even realize it?"

Emily was Rhys's ex-wife, and though they'd been divorced for many years, they had remained good friends. It wasn't quite like being a recent widower, but it was close.

"Is it too simplistic to suggest taking it one day at a time? Rhys is a good man, Wendy. He won't intentionally hurt you."

Removing her necklace, she whispered, "I know. It's just that I haven't felt this way about a man in a very long time."

She'd had a brief relationship with Gemma's boss, but I knew her feelings for him had never been this deep. *Thank goodness.* The man was an overbearing, obnoxious jerk.

"Wendy, it was you who chanted carpe diem when I fell for a man who lived across the pond. Even if it hadn't worked out, I think I can honestly say, I wouldn't have missed it for the world." I paused. "And you're known for throwing caution to the wind."

My words had the desired effect. She lifted her chin and smiled. "You're right. This isn't like me. I'm going to accept that Prince Charming has come to Astonbury to escort me to the ball and go from there."

For the rest of the afternoon, an image of Disney's Cinderella dancing with her prince flashed in and out of my brain. My prince would be absent, but I could live vicariously.

Tonight, the stone pillars that flanked the entrance to Astonbury Manor were topped with Christmas trees with tiny white lights. As I drove up the driveway, I saw a parking area set up to the right and two horse-drawn carriages. *Oh my goodness, Ellie's done it again.*

It was a tradition that Ellie's birthday was celebrated the night after the tree lighting, and I'd learned that she added a different touch every year. We'd been greeted by footmen in front of the manor house last year. Tonight, as I was helped into a carriage, I felt as though I was stepping into a fairy tale.

Music from *The Nutcracker* filled the air as I took the footman's hand to alight at the front steps. Lifting my black satin skirt, I hurried up the stairs. A strapless satin dress wasn't made for the chilly evening air, even when topped with a cape.

Hearing my name, I turned to see Wendy waving as she and Rhys emerged from the library. There was no way I was letting Rhys get away with the requisite kiss on the cheek. I snaked my arm around his waist and pulled him into a hug. "I'm so glad you're here."

"I wouldn't have missed it. Wendy and I were discussing New Year's in London and wondering whether you and Dave would join us." As we chatted about the possibility, Wendy caught my eye and winked. I took that to mean she'd set her concerns aside.

From there, I wandered into the library. Like the other rooms, this one was decked in greenery. Belle and Peter were standing in front of an easel chatting with Ellie. Tall and athletic, Peter towered over the two women. When he stepped aside, I realized the easel held a painting of Ellie with her corgi, Blanche. *This must be Lucy's work.*

Belle lifted her hand and beckoned to me. "Leta, you have to see this."

Ellie chimed in to say that it was an early birthday present from Sarah and Matthew. "I'm delighted with how well she captured Blanche's impish spirit. I understand she'll be doing a portrait of Dickens and Christie, too. Goodness, before you know it, the entire village will have a Lucy Miller portrait."

At dinner, I was seated between Toby and Sam, who were both lively conversationalists. I heard about Sam's Cambridge studies and Toby's flourishing business. As I made my way through the five-course meal, I thanked my lucky stars I was cycling with Peter the next day. My ears perked up when I heard Sam mention Buttercup. "She what?"

Sam frowned. "She crossed the river and showed up at the Olde Mill Inn. I thought Mum was going to shoot me, since I was supposed to be watching her. When Libby called, I fetched the bedraggled thing and brought her home for a bath."

"I tell you what, Sam, tomorrow after my bicycle ride, I'll talk to your mum about letting Buttercup stay with me. My garden is small enough that I won't lose sight of her, and I can take her on walks with Dickens. We don't need another lost dog in the village."

Toby joined the conversation. "You're right, Leta, but the good news is that Constable James's sister got her dog back. Someone found him in the churchyard."

"Was he okay? It's been cold and damp, and he's been gone nearly a week."

"Jonas said he was fine, and that makes him all the more convinced someone took him, but the little thing got away."

Strange. Wasn't it more likely he wandered away and someone took him in?

CHAPTER FIVE

THE NEXT DAY, I called Sarah after I returned from cycling with Peter. She was relieved and grateful that I was willing to take Buttercup. "I tell you, Leta, I don't know what's going on with her. Right now, she seems tuckered out, and she's not eating. Maybe it's a combination of her river adventure and then a bath. Let me hold on to her, and if she doesn't perk up, I may take her to the vet Monday. If I can be sure there's nothing wrong with her, I'll take you up on your offer."

"No worries, Sarah. She and Dickens get along well."

My ride had worn me out, and my knee ached. I never knew what would set it off. It could have been a night in heels, or a long bicycle ride, or some combination. I grabbed an ice pack from the freezer and propped my leg on the ottoman. As I leaned my head back on the sofa, I realized I hadn't stopped since 6:30 a.m. No wonder I was tired.

Dickens, on the other hand, was full of energy. He placed his paws on my thigh. "Leta, can we play ball? Can we see the donkeys?" If I was going to take him for a walk, I needed to do it before I dozed off. Once I got comfortable, it would be difficult to get fired up about more exercise.

"Christie, it's pretty chilly out there. Shall we leave you behind?" She made her wishes known by rolling over and stretching out in front of the fireplace.

After replacing the ice pack with a knee brace, I was as ready as I was going to be. Dickens and I crossed to the other side of Schoolhouse Lane, and Watson appeared from out of nowhere. He strolled along beside Dickens, and I picked up snippets of their conversation. Watson was full of the news about Buttercup. "Did you hear she crossed the river?"

"Why? Do you think she was looking for Lucy?"

Watson seemed to think so. I heard him meow something about Buttercup wanting her mum. *Poor thing.* Maybe she was worried that Lucy had left her for good, just as Tanya had. The subject changed to donkeys as they trotted toward us, and it wasn't long before Watson darted through their enclosure and disappeared.

Later that evening, a text came in from Sarah. "Taking Buttercup to the vet in the morning. Still not eating. Will call you tomorrow."

Could she be depressed? Is that a thing in dogs? I was pondering that when my phone rang.

Dave's cheerful voice greeted me. "Hi there, sweetheart. Haven't heard a peep from you today. Are you still recovering from your big night out?"

"More like a big night and a strenuous bicycle ride with Peter. Oh, and a walk with Dickens. How's your day been?"

I wanted to be distracted by our banter, but I couldn't get my mind off Buttercup. As was so often the case, Dave detected something in my voice. "You sound more preoccupied than tired. Is there something else going on?"

"Well, yes. It's Buttercup."

After I shared the story, he commented that we'd seen the same thing with the corgi who belonged to Emily. "Remember, Wimsey was subdued after she died. Maybe you should ask Rhys how he's doing now. By the way, thanks for the photos from the party. It was nice to see Rhys and Wendy enjoying themselves. Of course, though, my favorites were your selfies. Almost made me want to hop a plane."

"Flattery will get you everywhere, you know." He had succeeded in making me smile, something he was very good at.

Christie and I were walking in the door from yoga when Sarah called. "If you're still up for taking Buttercup, I'll bring her over now. The vet prescribed anti-depressants for her, and we're about thirty minutes away."

"Oh, I'm so glad she's not sick. Come on over. Dickens and I will cheer her up."

Quite often, Christie was feisty and sarcastic, but at times like this, she could be sweet. "Hey, what about me? I can help too."

After I let Dickens in, we three arranged ourselves on the floor in front of the fire. Christie sat in my lap, seeming to listen attentively, while Dickens lay by my side. "The best I can tell, Buttercup misses Lucy. Maybe this is the longest Lucy has left her and she doesn't understand that Lucy will be back. I'm not sure, but our job is to keep an eye on her, cheer her up, and get her to eat."

Dickens's thoughts on eating cracked me up. "She's not eating? Are you sure she's not sick?" My boy was all about food, so the idea that someone would miss a meal was shocking to him.

Christie's reaction was practical. "She can share my food—if you can keep Dickens out of it."

"Right, more like she can share it after it's been in your dish for more than two minutes, and it's no longer acceptable to you."

It was good to see their hearts were in the right place. I bustled about pulling out an old blanket and an extra food bowl in preparation for our guest, and when Sarah pulled up in the driveway, we were ready.

Buttercup was a bit wobbly getting out of the
Jeep, but Sarah explained the vet thought that came
from lack of food. The pills he'd prescribed were
to be given with Buttercup's evening meal, and if
I could get her to eat before then, all the better.
He said socialization and exercise would help too.
Standing in my driveway with her head tilted, she
looked forlorn.

I held onto her collar as Sarah backed out,
and then I ushered Buttercup inside, where she
followed Dickens to the sitting room and lay down
in front of the fire. All afternoon, I plied her with
kibble. She would intermittently eat a bite or two
and then rest her head between her paws and gaze
into the fire. Dickens lay beside her, and Christie
got into the act by snuggling against Buttercup's
head and playing with her ears.

When her demeanor hadn't changed by late
afternoon, I decided that a walk to see Martha and
Dylan might do the trick. The sun would soon set,

so I hurried to get everyone ready—not a simple task when I required a knee brace in addition to my parka and gloves.

With dog leashes in hand, I opened the kitchen door, only to hear a last-minute demand from Christie. "Take me too."

"Hold on! This is turning into a three-ring circus." I looped the two leashes around my neck, turned around to get Christie's backpack, and bedlam broke out. Buttercup, who'd been nearly comatose all day, darted out the door. Dickens chased after her. Christie ran between my legs. And I went down.

The next few minutes were a blur. I hobbled to my feet, calling for the dogs, and stumbled outside. Christie was positioned at the end of the driveway, screeching, "Come back."

My first thought was that they'd run to the neighbor's yard where they could cut through to get to Astonbury Manor, but there was no sign of them across the street. I looked to the left, thinking the donkeys might have been an enticement, but I glimpsed brake lights across the bridge and nothing else.

Where have they gotten to so quickly? When I heard a horn coming from the direction of the High Street, I had my answer. That sound was followed by the slamming of car doors and loud voices. By now, my neighbor Deborah had emerged from her cottage and was headed toward the street.

She stopped at the end of her driveway and looked both ways, her hand shading her eyes. "What on earth?"

We came together between our cottages. There were no dogs in sight and no cars, though I thought I heard a motor out of sight around the bend. "Deborah, did you see Dickens and Buttercup?"

"No. I heard a commotion—you calling the dogs, a car horn, and doors slamming." She pointed at my knee brace. "You stay here, I'll run up toward the High Street to see what 's going on."

As she took off, I grabbed the keys from my pocket and got in my car. "I'll be back, Christie. Don't go anywhere."

I caught up to Deborah just past the gates to Astonbury Manor, where Schoolhouse Lane curved toward the High Street. She came to the car, and we both looked up toward the intersection. The streetlights were coming on, and a few people were strolling toward the village green. "Leta, I didn't see the dogs or a car. Do you want me to come with you to check near the shops?"

"I know you need to get back to Timmy. If you'll put Christie inside, I'll drive around. I'm sure the sound came from this direction, aren't you?"

"I think so, but it can't hurt to make the loop and check at the other end near the donkey barn. It's not like Dickens to take off, is it? What happened?"

I told her I'd explain when I got back and slowly made my way to the intersection. I glanced up and down the street before taking a left. The street was relatively quiet. There was a yoga class going on in Rhiannon's studio. Toby's Tearoom would be closing soon but still had a few customers inside, and Tommy and Tuppence were reclining in the front window of the Book Nook.

Doing a U-turn, I drove toward the village green. It was a picture-postcard scene—the streetlights festooned in their red bows and greenery, the twinkling lights of the Christmas tree, the white lights on the Village Hall. All was well in the village of Astonbury—except I'd lost two dogs.

I crossed the bridge over the River Elfe and continued to where Schoolhouse Lane pulled off to the right. Should I turn toward my cottage or the donkey barn and the Olde Mill Inn? *Where are they?* I could only hope they weren't trotting up the road to Bourton-on-the-Water, where the traffic would begin to get heavier. Choosing the right turn, I crossed the smaller bridge over the river and pulled into my driveway.

Deborah opened the door as I climbed from my car. "No luck? I kept hoping they'd show up before you returned. That's why Timmy and I are here. We made a pot of tea."

Timmy looked up from his drawing pad and crayons. "Hi, Leta. I'm making you a picture."

Dropping into a chair at the kitchen table, I put my face in my hands. "What am I going to tell Sarah, much less Lucy? And what got into Dickens?"

"Tell me what you're doing with Buttercup in the first place?" She placed a welcome cup of tea in front of me.

As the story tumbled out, Deborah listened attentively. "I wonder what caught Buttercup's attention. Did the car we heard pass by here first? Did she think it was Lucy?"

"I don't know what to think. Whatever the reason for it, her habit of running off is nerve-wracking, and I should have put the leash on her before I ever opened the door. What was I thinking?"

"It sounds like you would have been fine if you hadn't decided to go back for Christie."

Christie hopped in my lap. "She's not blaming me, is she?"

"No Christie, it's all my fault. I was careless."

Deborah gave me a bemused look. "You mentioned Christie darting between your legs. What got into her?"

"Who knows? Maybe she knew the dogs were up to no good."

Timmy looked up. "Cats are smart. Spot would have known, and I bet Christie did too." *Out of the mouths of babes.*

My young neighbor handed me his drawing. It was a red Christmas stocking with a black cat peeking from it. "This is for you and Christie—to keep you company until Dickens comes home."

As I thanked him, Deborah ruffled his hair. "That was thoughtful. Let's you and me check with the Morgans across the street. Maybe they saw something." She stood. "You're going to post something on the *Astonbury Aha*, right, Leta? Now that I think of it, I've seen a few lost dog postings over the past few weeks."

"Exactly my plan, but only after I call Sarah."

It was all I could do to hold it together to call Sarah. I barely got the words out of my mouth before she reacted. "Oh my gosh, Leta. I'll send Sam out to drive the estate. Maybe they're wandering here."

"I am so, so sorry, Sarah. You entrusted Buttercup to me, and now this."

"Stop it, Leta. She could have run off when I unloaded her from the car earlier. Something's up with her for sure. I'm the one who should be sorry because now Dickens is missing too."

There was a tiny part of me that agreed—not that Sarah should be sorry, but that Dickens would never have run off on his own. *What could have gotten into him? What will I do if he doesn't come back?*

Sarah decided it would do no good to tell Lucy at this juncture because there wasn't anything she could do from France, and I agreed. I thought back to when Henry and I traveled overseas and left Dickens's elderly predecessor with my sister. Anna and I had an agreement that if anything happened to Banjo while we were gone, she wouldn't tell us until we got home. Thankfully, nothing ever did.

Hanging up, I scrolled through the pictures on my cell phone until I found the one of Dickens and Buttercup in their new collars. I posted a lost dog alert on the *Astonbury Aha* with their photo and last known location. Almost as an afterthought, I added a note about a reward.

Next, I called Wendy. My voice broke on the words "Dickens and Buttercup ran off." That was all my friend needed to hear before she said she was on her way.

While I waited, I sent an email to my friends along with the photo and asked them to be on the lookout for the two rogue dogs. It seemed like only minutes before responses started flying in. Barb Peters replied she would print my email and post it on the door to the Ploughman Pub and put copies on the bar. Beatrix said Trixie would work up a poster and print copies for the village shops to post in their windows. When Toby saw her response, he asked for fifty copies so he could hand them out in the morning. Libby said she would alert Gemma and Jonas.

I was wondering what else I could do when Wendy knocked and opened the door. Her brother stood quietly behind her as she told me the plan. "I stopped by the garage, and Peter suggested we ride around the village looking for them. They can't have gone far, can they?"

"I don't know what to think. Dickens has never run off before."

Peter knelt to pet Christie, who was twining around his ankles. "Right, but Buttercup has done it at least twice that we know of. Once to your driveway and once to the inn. Maybe she's a bad influence."

Christie leaped to the kitchen table and meowed. "Leta, I bet Dickens is trying to get her to come home. You told us we needed to watch out for her."

Great, another thing to lay at my door. Dickens had been my little hero dog more than once, and if he felt responsible for Buttercup, he could be trying to keep her from harm's way, much as he did with me.

"Maybe Christie's right—I mean, I mean, listening to her meow is making me think. Maybe Dickens is following Buttercup, trying to keep her safe." It was a sign of how stressed I was that I'd almost let the cat out of the bag, so to speak. "Maybe Buttercup is hurt, and he won't leave her."

I explained that she'd barely eaten anything for two days. "She seemed lethargic—until she bolted from the yard. It was like she suddenly had a shot of vitamin B-12."

Wendy put her hands on her hips. "Look, we can stand here talking about why they took off, or we can do something. I say we ride around looking for them. Peter can drive, and you and I can lean out the windows watching for them and calling Dickens. I think he's more likely to respond to your voice."

I didn't have a better idea, so that's what we did. We drove nearly to Bourton with the windows rolled down, calling for Dickens. Peter had a powerful flashlight, so we shone it on one side of the road on the way up and on the other on the way back.

We couldn't think of anything else to do after that, so we went to the Ploughman to grab dinner. My knee had stiffened on the ride, and I nearly fell from the truck when Peter opened my door. "Blimey, Leta, we need to get some ice on that."

He helped me inside and seated me at a table while Wendy stopped by the bar to order cider. When I propped my leg on a chair, I groaned. "It's not a good sign that I can already see the swelling." Taking off my shoe, I unstrapped the brace, tugged it off over my foot, and rolled my yoga pants above my knee. It was not a pretty sight.

Wendy sat our beers on the table and gingerly touched my puffy black and blue knee. "I'll be back with ice."

It was a quiet night in the pub. The weekenders were gone, and things wouldn't pick up again until Thursday. Astonbury's holiday lights weren't as elaborate as those in Bourton-on-the-Water or nearby Broadway, but we got our share of holiday visitors.

When Wendy returned with a bag of ice wrapped in a towel, she draped it over my knee and pushed my pint closer to my hand. "Drink. I ordered Peter his usual burger, and fish and chips for the two of us. This is not a night for thinking of diets."

All I could do was stare morosely into my pint. Peter patted my hand. "Leta, I'll take my bicycle out in the morning and ride the loop on the other side of the village."

Nodding glumly, I looked at my leg. "If I weren't one of the walking wounded, I could cycle to Bourton. You see things differently from a bicycle than you do from a car. There could be a shed or a barn along the way, somewhere they might have spent the night to stay warm."

"*If* they're on their own," Wendy said. "I hate to say this, but Rhys mentioned there'd been a rash of dognapping in London. He doesn't let Wimsey out unless he can stand and watch him."

Peter gave his sister a stern look. "But this isn't London, and Rhys said they're brazen. They walk right into gardens and snatch the dogs. Dickens and Buttercup ran from Leta's cottage. They weren't snatched."

A solitary tear slid down my face. "I hadn't even considered that someone might have picked them up, except to keep them from getting hit by a car. I keep telling myself it was late when they took off today, and that by tomorrow, someone will have taken them to a vet to check their chips. They're both chipped."

Snatched or off on a doggie adventure. I had to believe those were the only alternatives, and that either way, someone would contact me—be it a dognapper or a good Samaritan. I couldn't allow myself to think the worst—that one or both of my furry friends were lying injured on the side of the road.

CHAPTER SIX

AFTER WENDY AND PETER dropped me off at
home, I took a long shower, thinking I'd call Dave
when I was done. I wanted to hear his voice, but
I wasn't sure I could bear going through the story
again. In the end, I texted him the shortest possible
version and said I'd call in the morning.

Lying in bed with an icepack on my knee and
Christie tucked against my side, I tried to distract
myself with the December book club selection.
I'd read *How to Find Love in a Bookshop* several

years ago and wanted to refresh my memory for
Thursday night's discussion, but it was no use.
After rereading the same page several times, I gave
up and turned out the light.

By 2 a.m., when I was no closer to sleep, I gave
in and called Dave. "I wondered whether you'd be
able to sleep," he said.

"It seems not. Between worrying about Dickens
and Buttercup and icing my swollen knee, I'm
miserable."

"Your knee? What did you do this time?"

And so, the story poured out. "I don't know,
Dave, I just don't know. I'm trying not to think the
worst, but—"

"Whoa. Take a deep breath, sweetheart. You're
probably right that someone saw them trotting
along the road and took them home, and you'll get
a call in the morning. Maybe worst-case scenario,
they're tucked away somewhere on the estate and
will come out looking for breakfast."

"I hope so. Tell me about your day. Did you mix packing with writing?"

"Yes, a little of both. As you pointed out, I can't manage to put a book in a box without flipping through it. That makes for slow going. And the stack of books coming with me seems to be getting bigger."

That made me laugh. He'd easily decided that his furniture was going to Goodwill, but books were a different matter—not that I had any room to talk. I had a built-in bookcase that spanned an entire wall in my office, and it was filled to the gills. The two that flanked the fireplace in the sitting room at least had a few shelves dedicated to knickknacks.

"Maybe what I should get you for Christmas is a bookshelf. I can think of a couple of spots where we could fit one in. I'll call the man who built the ones I have now and see what he thinks."

We continued in that vein for a few minutes until I yawned. Dave chucked. "I heard that. Why don't you try to get some sleep now, and I'll call you tomorrow when I wake up?"

When my phone rang Tuesday morning at 7 a.m., I was sound asleep. I fumbled for it, knocked it off my bedside table, and managed to answer it before it went to voicemail. Not before nearly standing on my head to find it on the floor, though. "Hello."

"Is this Leta Parker?"

"Yes, are you calling about the dogs? Have you seen them?"

"No, sorry, I haven't, but my dog went missing not long ago. The good news is he's back home, but when I saw your post about your two, I thought you might want to hear how I got him back. I hesitated to call this early, but I'm on my way to the train station, and wanted to be sure I got you."

Squirming into an upright position in bed, I asked the man on the other end of the line to continue. He introduced himself as Bob Weir. "Well, the first thing you need to know is that I travel to London most weeks, usually Tuesday through Thursday. I'm fortunate that my neighbor Margaret looks after Bingo when I'm gone.

"Like I did this morning, I let Bingo outside in the garden while I have breakfast and pack my gear for my commute. He comes in, and at midday, Margaret visits to let him out. Sometimes they take a short walk, but mostly she lets him wander the yard for thirty minutes or so. She goes back to her cottage and then returns to let him inside. She repeats that routine at dinnertime and again before she turns in for the night."

"How fortunate you are to have such a good neighbor."

He chuckled. "That I am. Margaret is quite attached to Bingo. But back to the story. Two weeks ago, she let him out at dinnertime, and he was nowhere to be found when she went to put him inside. The little scamp does sometimes nap beneath a bush where you can't see him, but not this time. Naturally, Margaret was frantic. She walked our lane searching for him, but he was gone. She even knocked on doors to see if anyone had seen him."

"Oh my gosh, she must have felt awful. What happened?"

"Well, of course, she called me and was so upset, I could hardly understand her. I was as worried as she was, but it wasn't her fault. She's followed the same routine for several years now, and there's never been a problem. Our plan was that she'd look for him again in the daylight and call the local dog shelters, and I'd post something on the *Astonbury Aha*."

"And someone found him?"

"Yes, but it was several days later. There'd been no phone calls, and I was beginning to think the worst. Especially because Bingo's a Jack Russell, and a co-worker told me that's a popular breed with dognappers."

Dognapping? Here? "What a horrible thought, but surely that only happens in the big cities."

"At the time, I had no idea, but I wondered about it later. And here's why. While I'm away, Margaret takes the post from the front hall and stacks it on my dining room table, and I don't get to it right away, sometimes not until Sunday. Fortunately, I sorted it Friday afternoon, and mixed in with the junk mail was an envelope addressed *Hello* with my address."

"Oh my gosh. Was it a ransom demand?"

"That was my first thought as I tore open the envelope. Inside was a piece of lined paper with cut-out letters from a magazine—straight out of a mystery book. But all it said was, 'Do you miss your dog?' No way for me to respond."

I was getting anxious just hearing his story. "Did you think of reporting it to the police?"

"Yes. I called the station, and they asked me to bring the envelope and note to them, that they couldn't free anyone up to come to me. I guess I understand that. To them, Bingo is only a dog. It's not like it was a missing person case, but it felt that way to me. I got right in my car and drove to Stow. I gave the officer at the desk the story and turned over the evidence. He advised me to call the Dog Warden and the Jack Russell rescue group too, and he brought up the possibility that Bingo might have been dognapped."

That word again. "And?"

"What you would expect. They said they'd be in touch if anything came of it. I went to bed thinking nothing would. I mean, what were they going to do? Dust it for fingerprints? But here's the thing. Saturday morning, I got a call from a bloke saying he'd found Bingo. He offered to bring him home, and in no time, I had my boy back."

"Oh my gosh. You must have been so relieved. Where did he find him?"

"He spotted him late Friday between here and Bourton. Said he saw a white blur as he rounded a curve and that my boy was a muddy mess. He took him home, gave him a bath, and fed him. It was just by chance that he saw my online post on Saturday morning. I had to push him to take £40 when he brought Bingo home—would've given him more if I'd had it on hand."

"Oh my goodness. He was missing all that time, and you got him back unharmed after what? Five days? If only someone sees Dickens and Buttercup."

"Yes, I hope your story has a happy ending too."

I was curious. "Thank you. Now tell me, please, do you live anywhere near where he was found?"

"Well, that's the thing. As the crow flies, it's about ten kilometers, but if he traveled by road, it's more like fifteen. Either way, it's a long way for Bingo to wander. He's no spring chicken, and I can't fathom how he got that far from home. And when I took him to the vet to be checked out, he hadn't lost a bit of weight. He's a plump little thing. So what was he living on?"

"That's a good question. Could someone else have been feeding him?" My wheels were turning, but Bob was way ahead of me.

"Well, you may think I'm crazy, but I'm wondering whether someone took him and decided they didn't want him after all, or whether maybe he got away."

Closing my eyes, I tried to make sense of what he was saying. "No, I don't think you're crazy, but I'm trying to understand. If someone went to the trouble to take him, why would they let him go?"

"It's the dognapping thing. If their aim was to make money, they were probably disappointed when they realized he was a senior citizen."

I followed his reasoning. "And it would be too risky or too much trouble to return him to his home, right?"

"Exactly. And I thought it odd that his collar was missing. I've never known him to wiggle out of it. Plus, Margaret and I have no clue how he got out of the garden. The whole thing strikes me as peculiar. Please don't get me wrong—I'm happy to have him home. I just can't help wondering where he was Tuesday through Friday."

He cleared his throat. "It's like a giant puzzle. As I mulled it over, I wondered if the note wasn't a set-up? Like maybe the lad who called me had him all along and primed the pump with the note, knowing I'd be so relieved when he showed up that I'd give him money. Do you think I've watched too much telly? Or does the sequence of events seem strange to you too?"

I tried to digest his various theories. It sounded like something Wendy and I would have come up with. One scenario was that someone snatched Bingo but let him go. Another was that someone saw him and fed him, but the senior dog continued to wander until he was rescued on the road. And then there was the more sinister idea that this was an elaborate plot to extract money from Bob.

"Are you there? You must think I'm crazy."

My imagination was working overtime. "No, I don't. It sounds like something I would think. A bit *Midsomer Murders*-ish, but plausible, except in Midsomer, there'd be a murder next. Or three. It seems there are always three murders in that show."

Despite the circumstances, we chuckled about being addicted to BBC mysteries. "Bob, thank you so much for calling. I plan to start contacting shelters today, and I think I'll touch base with the police. My friend Gemma is an inspector in Stow, and she may have some idea as to whether similar things have been happening around the area. By the way, do you know the name of the officer you spoke with at the station?"

"Hmm. James, Constable James, I think."

"Oh my goodness, did you know Constable James's sister lost her dog last week and someone found it in the churchyard? That's two missing dogs in a matter of weeks—not to mention my two."

"You're kidding! It's almost like I jinxed him. I sure hope your two show up."

My shoulders slumped. "Me too. The good news is they aren't pedigreed dogs, so I don't think dognappers will come into play. I'm worried enough that they've been gone overnight without thinking about that."

"I suspect you're right. Hopefully, they'll soon tire of their adventure and make their way home."

"Thank you, Bob, and thanks for taking the time to contact me. I plan to start calling shelters today, and I'll contact the Dog Warden too." I promised to let him know when we found Dickens and Buttercup—emphasis on when. No matter that he was now the second person to bring up dognapping, the fact was that no one had pulled into my driveway and stolen the two animals. They had run off.

Was I fooling myself? Would a dognapper want Dickens and Buttercup? Dickens might be a purebred Great Pyrenees, but he was a dwarf, and once upon a time, breeders put down dogs like him. I doubted anyone would dognap him unless they didn't know what they were doing. And Buttercup was a one-of-a-kind *cuteapotamus*.

Throwing back the bedcovers, I put my feet on the floor. The ice had reduced the swelling in my knee, but the color was now a lovely reddish-purple. When I saw my reflection in the bathroom mirror, I cringed at the black circles beneath my eyes.

Christie leaped to the sink. "Are we going to look for Dickens?"

"Yes, as soon as I figure out where to start. Maybe we'll drive to Ellie's and walk the estate. I wonder if Basil knows where they've gotten to."

Downstairs, I pressed the button for the coffee and waited impatiently for it to brew. It wasn't only coffee I was impatient about. I wanted to *do* something. Sitting around, waiting for someone to call or text about Dickens and Buttercup, was making me crazy.

As if in answer to my thoughts, a text came in from Peter. "I'm off to ride the village. Will stop by on the way home." I sent him a thank you and poured a mug of coffee. He'd be riding part of the way in the dark, as the sun wouldn't be up until nearly 8 a.m., but for Peter, this was nothing out of the ordinary. It would take a driving rain or ice on the roads to stop him from getting in his morning ride.

I was thankful we were back on an even keel. I'd missed his friendship, and this ordeal would have been much worse without his support. He had a gentle way about him, and both Dickens and Christie adored him.

"Christie, let's make a list." When she followed me to the office, I realized she'd been unusually quiet this morning. No indignant cries for milk, no huffy demands for me to fluff the food in her dish. Today, she was a comforting presence.

As I pulled out a notepad, she leaped on the desk and knocked a pencil, a pen, and some paper clips to the floor. Yes, she was sweet, but she was still my mischievous girl. "Do you want treats, or do you want to continue clearing my desk?"

"Both," she meowed, as she reached her paw toward the mug that held my pens. The treats distracted her, and she was soon curled on the desk, watching me scrawl my ideas.

"We need to attack this from all angles, Christie. I'll pick up flyers from Beatrix and put them in letterboxes around the village. I should take some to the vets in Bourton and Stow and maybe Cheltenham. Posh Pets would be a good place too, and as soon as they open, I'll call the local animal shelters. Maybe I can email them the information."

Christie was focused on my moving hand, and in a flash, her paw came down on the page. "I keep telling you that the ink isn't like a string, Christie. You can't grab it."

She meowed, "You say that, but I'll get it one day." Rolling on her side, she stretched. "We should talk to Watson when we visit Basil. We need to find out what they both know."

"Watson! That's a spectacular idea. That cat gets around, and so does Paddington. That means we should stop by the inn too." I stared out the picture window to the garden. "What else? Oh! I need to find Constable James. He'll want to help, whether it's officially or unofficially."

With a limit to what I could accomplish before folks were awake and businesses open, I opted for breakfast and treated myself to cheese grits and scrambled eggs. I kept seeing Dickens out of the corner of my eye and had to stop myself from placing my breakfast plate on the floor for him to lick, something he always got to do before I washed up. My rule was no chunks to gobble, only a lick.

Peter startled me when he knocked on the door. Removing his helmet, he shook his head when I let him in. "Sorry, Leta. Didn't see hide nor hair of 'em. If I'm not too busy at the garage later, I'll cycle toward Bourton. And, when you get the flyers from Beatrix, could you drop some by? I can hand them out to customers."

When I read my list to him, he agreed that I'd covered all the bases before hugging me and hopping on his bicycle. I thought of Wendy saying that between the two of us, we'd transformed her brother into a hugger—a trait you didn't find in most Brits. She'd lived in North Carolina for so long before returning home to England that hugging came naturally to her, and quite a few of our close friends in Astonbury had adopted the gesture—only with the two of us, though. I'd yet to see them hug anyone else as Southerners do with just about everyone we encounter.

On the off chance Beatrix was in early, I called the Book Nook and was in luck. Trixie answered the phone. "I'm so sorry to hear about Dickens and Buttercup, Leta. I've got the flyers ready, and Toby already has his. If you'd like, I can run them over to you before we open."

I took her up on her offer and thanked her profusely. Next, I called Sarah. "Hi, I'm sorry to say there's no news."

"Oh, Leta. I was hoping against hope you'd say they'd turned up. I'll get Sam and Matthew to keep an eye out. Can you think of anything else I can do from here?"

When I shared my list, she offered to call the shelters, so that was one less thing for me to do. "Sarah, it's probably silly, but I think I'll come over and walk part of the estate on my own. They could be anywhere."

She assured me I could walk to my heart's content, and if I wanted her to, she'd get her stockwoman to take me around in the jeep. "You know Susan's out all day tending to the sheep, and she'd be happy to take you with her. Given your bum knee, you can't possibly explore everywhere on foot."

She was off to deliver her products to shops in Shrewsbury and neighboring villages like Ludlow and would be gone most of the day. We agreed I'd call Ellie if I wanted to ride the estate. As I worked through my list, my conversation with Bob Weir kept surfacing. I was sure Dickens and Buttercup had left on their own, but I wondered whether there was something I was missing. What I needed was someone to brainstorm with, and the best person for the job was Wendy. Who better than a member of the Little Old Ladies' Detective agency?

When I rang her, she was eager to jump in. "You know Mum wants to help, but I'm not sure what she can do. It's not as if her little old lady act can help in this situation. Are there phone calls she can make?"

"Well, Sarah's calling the shelters, but Belle could call the vets and Posh Pets. It would be a big help and make her feel useful at the same time. What I need most from you is your brainpower. How 'bout I text a copy of my list for you to ponder while I'm at Astonbury Manor? And then, could you ride with me to Bourton and Stow to post the flyers?"

Having Wendy by my side would keep me from falling apart as the day progressed. I knew that the longer I went with no word, the more distraught I would get. Fingers crossed someone would contact me with good news before the day was out.

I was pulling out Christie's backpack when the phone rang. Since the initial call from Bob Weir this morning, each text or call made my pulse quicken with a combination of hope and fear. Would it be good news?

After I said hello, I heard the familiar voice of Constable Jonas James. "Leta, I called the first chance I had. I'm so sorry about Dickens. Have you had any word?"

The background noise told me he was calling from the station in Stow. "I'm manning the front desk this morning, so it's not easy to talk, but I'll try." He asked lots of questions as I explained what had transpired since yesterday afternoon. "I'm glad Mr. Weir got in touch, Leta. This may not be the same at all, but we should put our heads together."

He explained that it was Bob's case that had made him fear the worst when his sister's dog went missing. "I understand that Dickens and Buttercup took off from your driveway on their own, but after that, someone may have picked them up. And they may demand a ransom, if they contact you at all."

I had to think through what he was saying. *What does he mean, at all?* I thought it would be good news if someone picked them up and they weren't running along a busy road. And, if that someone wanted a ransom, I'd pay it, no matter how much they wanted.

"Jonas, you know, don't you, that money is no object when it comes to getting Dickens back? That's why I offered a reward."

"Yes, Leta, I do. But there are other scenarios. Let's hope someone picks them up and contacts you right away so you can bring them home."

"Exactly."

"But let me lay out the other possibilities. One is the ransom scenario. Two, someone could pick them up with good intentions but decide they want to keep them. Three, they may have bad intentions from the get-go and want to sell them."

"Sell them? They're mutts—adorable mutts, for sure—not pricey pedigreed animals. Who would buy them?"

There was silence on the line before Jonas cleared his throat. "Leta, I hate to say this, but dognappers take adorable mutts and sell them to dogfighting rings or medical research facilities."

An image of Dickens in a ring with a vicious dog flashed through my mind. "Surely not."

As I was trying to shake my feeling of horror, Jonas rattled off the statistics. "Leta, nearly 2,500 dogs are stolen each year throughout England. That's close to seven a day. I looked it up when my sister's dog disappeared. One report estimated that a dog is stolen every five hours. And there are indications that organized gangs are beginning to see family pets as easy money."

He added that dognapping was only a property crime in the eyes of the law, meaning criminals might be fined but not locked up. If I wasn't alarmed before, I was now. Jonas must have sensed the impact his words were having. "Leta, I'm sorry. I didn't mean to scare you, but I wanted to drive home how serious this could be. I know the LOLs haven't handled a missing dog case, but if there was ever a time, it's now."

"But Jonas, dognapping doesn't happen here, does it? I mean, in the Cotswolds? That sounds like London or maybe Birmingham, right?"

"Yes, it's more prevalent in the big cities, but I'm seeing a disturbing pattern here, and Bob Weir's situation is part of it. My sister had an envelope in her letterbox too."

"What? What did hers say?"

"It wasn't exactly the same. It read, 'Do you miss Tank?'"

"Tank? I saw the picture of him online. That little thing is called Tank?"

He chuckled. "It was my dad's idea of a joke. My sister got him when he was a puppy, and she was still living at home. She wanted to call him Buttons because of his dark brown eyes, but Dad called him Tank from the get-go, and the name stuck. And that's the tale of how a tiny Yorkie got the name of Tank."

Distracted by that cute story, it took me a moment for my mind to return to the note. When I asked about it, he told me that, like Bob's, it consisted of letters cut from a magazine, and there was no information on how to contact the sender. Then, a day later, his sister got a phone call from someone who claimed he found Tank in the churchyard in Astonbury.

"I didn't know about the phone call until it was all over. She told the lad to come right over, and he said he would when he got home from work. Funny, it was a young girl who showed up, but just like Mr. Weir did, my sister gave her money—except it was only £20. She was overjoyed to get Tank back. And my four-year-old niece? She was over the moon."

I wanted to focus on the ransom and reward scenarios, but my brain kept veering to the horrid idea that Dickens and Buttercup might be sold to someone else.

"Leta, did I lose you?"

"Sorry, Jonas, I was trying to process everything you said. It's a lot to take in. Are you suggesting the LOLs investigate lost dogs? That unearthing the facts surrounding other cases could help us find Dickens and Buttercup?"

"I guess I am. I can provide the list of cases reported to us here in Stow—that would give you data on Broadway, Blockley, Bourton, and neighboring villages—but Gemma will have my guts for garters if she thinks I'm spending police time to investigate every lost dog posted online or in the local papers. And I may be able to throw in an hour here or there to probe further if you come up with anything."

He explained that December was a hectic time, what with the shoplifting and other petty crimes that increased with the throngs of holiday tourists. Add in trying to arrange schedules so everyone got time off with their families, and it was the perfect storm.

"Picking up the list is easy, since Wendy and I will be in Stow this afternoon to post flyers. I'm not sure I have it in me to investigate lost dog cases while I'm scouring the area hoping to catch sight of my wayward boy and his companion, but I'll think about it. Belle and Ellie would be happy to make a few phone calls, though. And, Jonas, thanks for thinking of me and Dickens."

I imagined him ducking his head and blushing. He had a good heart. *Now, where is Christie?*

My unspoken question was answered when Christie meowed, "Can we go now? We need to find Dickens!" Detective Christie was on the case.

CHAPTER SEVEN

THE WALK TO ASTONBURY Manor was one I
liked to take with Dickens, but my knee meant
that wasn't an option this morning. I strapped the
backpack in the back seat, drove the short way, and
parked by the front entrance.

Caroline, the household chef, answered my
knock. "Oh, Leta, tell me you've found those
precious pups."

As she ushered me to the kitchen, I explained I'd
come to search the estate. Ellie was ready with a

mug of coffee when I removed my backpack and unhooked Christie.

"We're here to look for Dickens and Buttercup," Christie meowed.

Blanche barked from beneath the table, "They like the sheep barn, you know. I stay away from there because Ellie doesn't like for me to get dirty."

I smiled at Ellie's dog. Blanche avoided the sheep barn because she preferred to romp indoors and chase balls on the wooden floors with Dickens. Before Buttercup's arrival, Basil was Dickens's only outdoor companion.

When Caroline offered me fresh-baked bread with homemade blackberry jam, I made a half-hearted attempt to decline but failed. It was still warm, and the first bite was heavenly. "Goodness, Caroline, take it away before I eat the entire loaf. I never was any good at making bread, which is probably a good thing. It's bad enough that I can't live without pasta."

Caroline tilted her head. "But I hear you're a dab hand at making a Greek salad."

We three avoided the elephant in the room for a few minutes. It was Christie who prompted me to get down to business when she meowed, "Where's Watson?"

I realized he hadn't visited us the night before nor this morning, and that was odd. His routine was to hang around my kitchen door and stroll inside to visit Christie when I let Dickens out first thing in the morning, and again before I went to bed. What he did during the night was anyone's guess. As for the daytime hours, he occasionally surprised us with a visit, like he had when he told us about Buttercup crossing the river. He was the animal version of the town crier.

Locating the friendly tabby could come later. "Ellie, I spoke with Constable James this morning, and he suggested an unusual case for the Little Old Ladies' Detective Agency."

As I'd been, she was intrigued by the tale of notes composed of letters cut from magazines. We both wondered what would have followed if the missing canines hadn't been spotted and returned by kind villagers.

Spreading jam on another slice of bread, Ellie asked my opinion. "Do you think there's anything to the idea Bingo's owner had? That the note was planted to scare him and make him inclined to generously reward whoever showed up with his dog?"

"Honestly, Ellie, I don't know what to think. Bingo is a Jack Russell, and he'd likely be worth more than £40 on the black market. I have no idea, though, what it takes to sell a dog that way. Since all dogs in England are required to be chipped, a buyer would have to be unscrupulous not to ask for papers. But then, I guess that's what the black market is all about. Clandestine buying and selling."

"True. There's the ransom angle, though. If the first note was followed with a demand for, say £150, the dognapper could make a fair amount running this scheme repeatedly. More of a guaranteed return than hoping the happy owner would offer a tip or a generous reward."

"Uh-huh, but then there are the logistics of a ransom drop and dog return to consider. That involves a higher chance of getting caught. Aaargh, it takes me back to the concept of risk and reward."

Caroline had been listening. "If a dognapper sent the note, how did the rescuer or finder—whatever you call him—how did he come by the dog? A dognapper took Bingo and Tank, and managed to lose them both? How likely is that?"

That was a good question. A vision of the dognappers in Disney's *101 Dalmatians* came to mind. "Inept dognappers? I can see them dressed in black with matching caps."

Ellie pursed her lips. "If only they were that obvious. It's more likely they look like one of us. Anyway, Dickens and Buttercup weren't snatched, so I'm puzzled by Jonas's suggestion. How would investigating these other missing dog cases help you find our two rascals?"

"I'm having a hard time wrapping my brain around that idea. Maybe he's envisioning an opportunistic dognapper seeing the pair on the side of the road, picking them up, and voilà, a scheme is hatched."

I sat up straighter. "Wait a minute. That could be it. The LOLs digging into missing dog cases could kill two birds with one stone. We'd be doing a good deed if we identified a gang of dognappers, and doing that could be a kind of preemptive strike in the quest to find Dickens and Buttercup."

The corners of Ellie's mouth turned up. "Maybe we can make some poor little boy or girl's holiday happier by finding their missing pet. I'm sure

Jonas's little niece was heartbroken when Tank disappeared. With you and Wendy driving to various villages this afternoon, making phone calls would be a perfect job for the senior members of the team."

The conversation lifted my spirits no end. "Wonderful. Thank you, Ellie. I'll deliver the lists from Jonas later today. Now, it's time for me to search the grounds to see what I can find." I set my cup down and stood to leave.

Christie twined herself around my ankles. "Don't forget Watson."

"Um, Ellie, is Watson anywhere around?"

"Funny you should ask. I haven't seen him since Monday morning. It's not like him to be gone this long, though it's happened once or twice before. It makes me wonder whether he has another girlfriend in addition to Christie."

Looking from me to Ellie, Christie answered her. "He does *not*! He would never two-time me."

Suppressing a giggle, I spoke to Christie. "What's that you say, princess? No one compares to you?"

I tucked her in the backpack and drove to the equipment barn, where Susan Bremer greeted me. As stockwoman on the estate, she was responsible for the sheep. "Leta, are you ready to conduct a search? We'll follow Basil for a bit, and after that, we can check the more remote areas. If they're around here, we'll find them."

"Thank you, Susan. And can we stop by the artisan cottages along the way to see whether anyone's caught sight of the two?"

"Sure thing. Climb in."

I stopped to hug Basil and whisper in his ear. "Basil, have you seen Dickens and Buttercup?"

He put a big paw on my shoulder. "Not in a day or two, but if they're here, we'll find them. There are lots of places where they could be."

As she drove, Susan told me the herd was doing well. "Would you like to stop by the lambing barn while we're out? We don't have many births this time of year, but one of the Cotswold ewes gave birth to triplets the first of December."

"Oh, I'd love to see them. I think of the breed as Raggedy Ann sheep with their dreadlocks hanging around their faces."

"I know! Increasing the herd of gentle giants was the main goal Matthew set for me when I came on board in February. He already had a substantial number of Romneys but wanted more of the Cotswold Lions. They added three more last December, and the spring lambing season was a good one. These triplets are a special treat."

Basil was headed for the river but turned and followed the Jeep to the lambing barn. He went directly to the trio nestled in the hay by their mother. With Christie in her backpack, I knelt by the sleeping triplets. "Look, Christie, one of them is black."

She peered from the backpack. "I thought they were always white like Dickens."

Looking at Susan, I asked the obvious question. "Isn't it odd to have a black sheep?"

"Yes, it's caused by a recessive gene, but he's cute, isn't he? We named him Marley."

The connection to the phrase black sheep popped into my mind. "I am such a word nerd, I'll have to google black sheep to see how it came to mean something negative, as in the black sheep of the family."

"Two reasons, Leta. In the eighteenth and nineteenth centuries, the black fleece couldn't be dyed, so it was unacceptable for wool making. And then, as you might expect, some saw it as a sign of the devil."

I snapped a few pictures. "You never know, the triplets may wind up in one of my columns."

When we returned to the Jeep, Basil led the way to the river and then turned north. "He seems to have a plan as to how we should search," Susan said. "Then again, I've noticed that Buttercup often wanders this way."

Following Basil meant I had no worries that I'd miss Dickens or Buttercup. If they were anywhere on the estate, he'd spot them long before I would. This was the first time I'd visited the far reaches of the property, and I didn't realize that the stone wall that I passed on the road to Stow was its back border. To me, it was just another beautiful wall made of the golden Cotswold stone. *This place is huge.*

Susan pulled up to an iron gate in the back wall. "We use this gate when supplies for the farm or the brewery are delivered by a large lorry. It stays locked otherwise. Buttercup is such a wanderer, I wonder whether she's ever come this far back."

Leaving Christie in the Jeep, I walked to the gate, where Basil stood with his nose pressed between the iron bars. He barked. "I've seen her back here,

Leta. And I've caught her digging by the gatepost. I'm not sure why when she can leave by the front drive any time she wants."

Susan was too far away to hear me speaking to Basil, so I quizzed him. "When she visits the small cottages and comes back here, do you know if she's looking for something? Or is she just wandering?"

Sitting on his haunches, he replied, "I don't know for sure, but I think she misses someone named Tanya. She whines that name sometimes, and she gets restless whenever Lucy isn't here."

"Basil, Tanya was Buttercup's owner before Lucy, but Tanya died. Maybe Buttercup is lonely." I rubbed his head. "Is it possible she doesn't understand that Tanya isn't coming back?"

"I don't think so. We dogs know when someone dies."

I thought about Matthew's father, Ellie's husband, dying last year. "Did you and Blanche know that Nigel died without anyone telling you?"

"Yes, Leta, we did, and Blanche took it awfully hard because she spent lots of time with him."

As we walked along the wall, I heard the occasional car pass by on the road. Even off-leash, Dickens was good about staying on the verge when we walked, but would he do that without me by his side? I had no idea how Buttercup would behave on a busy road.

Susan cranked the Jeep when I climbed in. "Can you believe Basil? It's not exactly a grid search, but he's awfully thorough."

She was right. We followed him the length of the rear wall and down the tree line opposite the river. It wasn't long before he veered toward the brewery, and, as if he knew, he moved on to the cottages after that. Susan stopped at a few so I could ask the residents about the dogs.

The woodworker said he saw Buttercup every few days but couldn't say which ones, and the weaver had a similar recollection. The golden-haired dog

was a welcome sight when she came to visit, but no
one paid much mind to her schedule.

"What do you think, Leta? We've explored just
about every inch. Are you satisfied that Dickens
and Buttercup aren't here, or is there a spot you'd
like to revisit?"

I knew in my heart of hearts they were somewhere
else. One or both would have greeted us if they
were able, and if they were stuck or hurt, Basil
would have found them. "No, Susan. I think it's a
lost cause. It's time I focused on making calls and
putting up flyers. I have to believe someone's seen
them or taken them in, and I'll have them back
before long."

When she dropped me off at the equipment barn,
I headed to my taxi. "Christie, you've been quiet.
What do you think?"

"I think we need to ask Watson." It seemed that
Detective Christie had a one-track mind.

"Well, let's ask Basil if he's seen him." I called to him, and he came running.

Christie beat me to the punch. "Do you know where Watson is?"

Basil licked her face. "Haven't seen him today. Sometimes he tucks up in the lambing barn, but he wasn't there this morning. He could be across the river. You know how he likes those tree branches."

His river comment reminded me that I should check with Paddington about Watson and the missing duo. "Thanks, Basil, we'll stop there."

Christie wasn't happy when I dropped her off at the cottage. When I gave her a dab of wet food, she ignored her dish and meowed all the reasons why she should accompany me on my mission.

Tuning her out, I visited the front hall, where I found the thick envelope of flyers that Trixie had placed in the letterbox. The posters were on letter-size paper, and the photo was centered beneath the large heading—Lost Dogs. Trixie had

added the appropriate details under the colorful
picture. The words "Last seen on Schoolhouse
Lane Monday" were followed by "Reward" in all
caps. The last two lines contained my name, phone
number, and email address.

She'd left me a note that she had distributed the
poster to all the shops on the High Street and
left several in the Village Hall. She also planned to
contact the vicar at St. Andrew's Church to see if
he could post a few around the church. The girl was
a treasure.

Jenny had offered to help later in the afternoon
after the lunch rush at Toby's Tearoom. Together,
they would drive around Astonbury, placing flyers
in the letterboxes of the cottages on the outskirts
of the village. When they were done, everyone
in Astonbury would know that Dickens and
Buttercup were missing.

Texting Wendy that I was on my way to Sunshine
Cottage, I grabbed two bottles of water and shut

the door as Christie meowed, "Don't forget to check with Paddington."

The return text from Wendy informed me that Belle wanted to see me before we left for Bourton. I imagined she wanted to wish me well.

She did, but she also wanted to let me know she'd called the vets and Posh Pets. "Polly was terribly upset about the dogs and wanted me to be sure you were stopping by with flyers."

Wendy smiled at Belle. "Tell her the rest, Mum."

"Ellie's picking me up shortly, and we'll be camped out in her library all day going through the *Astonbury Aha* posts from the last month. We plan to note any mention of lost dogs or cats and contact the owners for an update. That way, when you bring us the list from Constable James, we'll be ahead of the game. "

I hugged her. "Thank you, Belle. That makes me think. I wonder whether there's a way to get back issues of the weekly papers in Bourton and Stow. Or do you think that's overkill?"

Wendy shook her head. "What if it is? If there's even a remote chance that collecting the information will help us find your boy, it will be worth it."

Belle smiled. "I love Ellie's idea that this could be a way to prevent future dognappings. If we have all this information at our fingertips, we may see a pattern—or a trail of breadcrumbs that leads us to the perpetrators. If it's one person or several people in cahoots, we may be able to put them out of business."

"A new tagline for the Little Old Ladies? You lose 'em, we find 'em? You and Ellie never cease to amaze me."

She sent us out the door with a tin of cookies to keep us fortified in our travels. As we approached the road, Wendy suggested we backtrack slightly to stop by the Ploughman. "Let's drop off flyers in time for the lunch rush here before we head to Bourton."

Barb was behind the bar. After Phil Porter's abrupt departure in September, the owners had promoted her to manager. She'd made subtle changes, starting with washing the windows. The place didn't sparkle, but it was noticeably brighter. And this was the first time that the pub sported holiday greenery around the windows and down the wooden posts on either side of the bar, courtesy of her cousin Brian, the local landscaper. Previously, a dusty string of artificial greenery topped the mantle, but that was it.

When she saw the flyers in my hand, she frowned. "I was hoping you had good news, but it's probably too soon. Hopefully, in the daylight, someone will spot them. Put a stack here on the bar, and I'll post one on the door in a moment."

There were a few lone cottages along the road to Bourton, and I pulled up long enough for

Wendy to hop out and stuff a flyer through the slots on the doors. As we approached the outskirts of Bourton-on-the-Water, where the cottages were closer together, I drove up and down a few side lanes for Wendy to hit those. In Bourton proper, we stopped by the tourism office, a few pubs, and a handful of shops. The owner of the small pet boutique offered to make more copies and pass them out to the neighboring shops. Everyone we encountered promised to be on the lookout and offered words of encouragement.

Wendy opened the tin of cookies for the umpteenth time and broke the last one in two. "It must be a sign of how stressed we are that these cookies are nearly gone. We're usually so disciplined."

Swallowing the last bite, I nodded. "My discipline has flown out the window on this emotional roller coaster. All the well-wishers lift my spirits, and then I think about Dickens and Buttercup being gone for nearly twenty-four hours, and the panic sets in."

CHAPTER EIGHT

In Stow-on-the-Wold, our first stop was the police station. A young female officer was at the front desk, and when I asked for Jonas, she explained he was working a split shift. "He's off until six, but he left you an envelope. I'm so sorry about your dogs."

I asked her if I could post a flyer on the bulletin board, and she looked around before suggesting I do it quickly. As I used a pushpin to stick the flyer on the cork, someone cleared their throat behind me.

"Leta Parker, is that what I think it is?" It was Gemma Taylor, Jonas's boss. She didn't sound happy.

Wendy gave her a defiant look. "Oh for goodness' sake, Gemma, please tell me this isn't against some constabulary rule."

Tugging at her ponytail, Gemma frowned. "No, it's not, but I'm already in hot water today over your lost dogs. I had to come to Constable James's defense when DCI Burton called me an hour ago." She lowered her voice. "The man can be such a git."

What? "Huh? What did Jonas do wrong?"

"Would you like to hear it verbatim? I quote, 'We do *not* investigate lost dogs, Detective Inspector Taylor.' He caught his constable in Stroud pulling together a list of missing dog reports to send here, and he read her the riot act before picking up the phone to give me an earful."

I wasn't surprised at DCI Burton's reaction. He'd proven himself to be a jerk on several occasions, but I was surprised at what he'd said. "Seriously, you don't ask your officers to be on the lookout?"

"Not officially, Leta. We want to be helpful, but no, we don't investigate. The one time we might have was when that gentleman in Astonbury got the strange note. But he'd only just turned it in when someone found his dog, so we dropped it. If it had been an honest-to-goodness ransom note, we might—emphasis on *might*— have pursued it."

My lips trembled. "I don't know whether to hope I get a note or not. I've offered a reward, and I told Jonas I'd pay anything to get Dickens and Buttercup back. At least if I got a note, I'd know someone had them, and they were safe. He scared me to death with his talk of dognappers."

Gemma placed her hand on my arm. "Leta, I know you're worried, but we have serious crimes to investigate."

Gritting my teeth, I struggled to form a response. I'd gotten along better with the prickly DI in recent months, but this unfeeling remark was more like the old Gemma. I wanted to throttle her. "Serious? This *is* serious to me."

She gave me a sheepish look. "That came out wrong. I don't mean to say this isn't serious, but it's not shoplifting or breaking and entering, and I can't have Constable James any more involved than he's already been. If you want to run something by him on the Q.T., that's fine, but please don't ask him to do any legwork for you."

Wendy must have realized I was at the end of my rope because she tugged me to the door and insisted we find lunch. It was a bit past the lunch hour, so we chose the pub at The Kings Arms, as much for its comforting log burner as for the food.

Splitting an order of fish and chips, we studied the contents of the envelope Jonas had left us. Only a handful of owners followed up with the station after initially reporting their animal missing. That meant there was no way of knowing whether they'd gotten their household pet back or not. With about twenty missing pets in the last sixty days, Belle and Ellie would have their work cut out for them following up with the owners.

Jonas had also included a copy of the Bob Weir note. It wasn't threatening, but it was unsettling. The day had turned misty, and I was tempted to linger by the fire, but my *work before play* trait spurred me to action.

When my phone rang, my first thought was that someone had seen the dogs, but it was Dave. It struck me that this could be the first time I was disappointed to see his name pop up.

"Hi, sweetheart, have you had any news?"

"Nothing encouraging. Instead, I had two very disturbing conversations—one with a man named Bob and another with Jonas."

When I went over the Bob Weir discussion,
his reaction was similar to what mine had been
initially. "Well, I guess the good news is both dogs
are lovable but not pedigreed, so hopefully this
dognapping thing isn't an issue."

"Yes, well, but then there's the call I got from
Jonas. He had more alarming information about
dognappers."

I gave him the gist of what Jonas had to say
and explained that I'd now enlisted Belle and Ellie
to investigate missing dogs. Wendy, meanwhile,
pulled out the police reports and gave him a few
highlights. "Dave, it *does* appear that most of
the dogs are pedigreed—Staffordshire bull terriers,
Yorkies, a German shepherd here and there. This
isn't an analysis, just what I see at a glance."

There was silence on the line, and I pictured him
running his hand through his dark hair. "So, the
information is encouraging in that so many are

pedigreed, but alarming when you think about the other reasons dogs are stolen."

I could tell he didn't want to say the words, so I did. "Yes, the dogfighting thing scares me to death."

Wendy hushed us both. "Okay, you two, enough of that. I think the most likely scenario is that the two rascals ran off. I don't know why they did, but that's what I think. I mean, Leta, you told me they bolted from the driveway, so I'm sticking with that. Someone will call soon."

I pictured a kind person stopping the car and exclaiming over the adorable duo before loading them in the car and taking them home. I imagined an older white-haired gentleman looking at Dickens's collar and calling me with the news. Why older? Who knows, other than it was a comforting image.

As we paid our tab, the bartender offered his assistance. "I couldn't help seeing your flyers, and I know how I'd feel if I lost my dog. Leave me a few to share with the locals, and at the check-in desk in the hotel. You never know who might have seen them."

From there, Wendy and I decided we'd split up. As we'd done in Bourton, we focused on spots that held the most promise—the pet boutique, the toy shop, and the bookstore. The vet was eager to help, and the tourist information center allowed me to post a flyer on the desk and the bulletin board before directing me to an office supply shop where I could make more copies.

As the clerk ran off the flyers, it occurred to me that extra copies of the police reports and the note to Bob Weir might also come in handy. At a minimum, I needed two sets to share with Belle and Ellie.

An older woman emerged from the back of the shop and stepped in to assist. "Let me help, luv." Pulling out binder clips, she sorted the copies into several sets and put them into a large cardboard envelope. "Now, you're good to go, and we'll take a poster for our door, too. Good luck to you."

When Wendy and I met in the square, we agreed we'd done everything we could in Stow. "Wendy, it's the other side of Astonbury from Sunshine Cottage, but do you want to accompany me to Posh Pets? I'd like to get some flyers to Polly."

She gave me a quick hug. "Sure. And maybe we'll think of something else we can do while we're on the road."

When we arrived at Posh Pets, Polly and Ric were in the middle of the room, working on dogs. Between blow dryers and razors, it was a noisy place. Mindy looked up expectantly from the front desk, but her expression quickly changed. "Oh no, you haven't heard anything yet? I'm so sorry."

Envelope in hand, I approached the desk. "I'm trying to believe that no news is good news, but the more time that passes, the harder it is."

She took a handful of flyers and pointed to the copy of the Bob Weir note. "What's this?" She turned it around to read. "Do you miss your dog? Huh?"

Once again, I explained the conversation with Bob and that I had enlisted the senior members of the Little Old Ladies' Detective Agency to work on missing dog cases. Polly stopped what she was doing and came to her mum's side. "That is so weird. Straight out of a mystery book, isn't it?"

Mindy looked at her daughter. "It reminds me of something, but I can't think what. Maybe something we watched on the telly?" The two chuckled about their BBC mystery addiction, and I told them I was a fellow addict.

By now, Ric had set his poodle client on the floor and walked over. "Still no sign of Dickens and Buttercup?" He glanced at the note. "And what's this?"

Wendy explained the note this time, probably thinking that one more time would send me over the edge. She also mentioned that despite what Bob and Jonas had said about dognappers, she was choosing to believe that the pair had run off of their own accord.

Tears pricked my eyes. "That's what I want to believe, too, but I'm awfully worried."

Ric looked from me to Polly. "I think we should take some flyers to Pepper's tonight. We can share them with the other volunteers so they can be on the lookout too. You've already called them, right, Leta, so they'll recognize Dickens and Buttercup if someone brings them?"

"Yes, we're on it, but that's a good idea about alerting the volunteers."

"Also, I'm a runner. I don't cover much territory, 10K on my daily runs, but I'll pay close attention. You get a different perspective on foot than you do in a car."

Mindy's eyes lit up. "They're bound to show up after their big adventure, Leta, and when they do, I bet they'll be a muddy mess. You bring them in here, and we'll clean them up free of charge."

The day was taking its toll, and it was all I could do to mumble a thank you as we left. In the car, I leaned my head on the seat. "I guess that's it, Wendy. Ready to go home?"

"Yes, and you look wrung out. Think you'll be able to sleep tonight?"

Before I could respond, my phone lit up with a call from an unknown number. "Hello."

A female voice responded. "Is this Leta Parker?"

"Yes. Are you calling about the dogs?"

"Yes. I think I may have seen the white one, but I can't be sure. My cottage is just over the River Elfe on the way to Bourton, and you must have put a flyer in my letterbox."

"Oh! When?"

"It was early this morning. I work at the hospital in Cheltenham, and I was on my way in when I caught a glimpse of white on the other side of the bridge. At the time, I didn't know whether it was an animal or a person, but it seemed to be climbing up from the river. When I found your flyer later, I thought it must be the dog named Dickens."

"Thank goodness. It gives me hope they're okay, or at least they were this morning. You're the only person so far to call me. Thank you so much."

"Well, I hope I'm right, and I'm sorry I can't tell you I saw the other one, but maybe that golden fur just didn't show up in the dark."

Wendy grasped my hand when I finished the call. "I told you they ran off. No dognappers in this story. Here's hoping the next caller says, 'They're eating me out of house and home. Come get them.' That would be your boy to a T."

My heart leaped when the phone rang a second time. This time it was Libby calling for an update.

When I told her about the call I'd just taken, she was encouraging. "That's great news. Sooner or later, those two will approach a cottage, I'm sure. They're bound to be hungry by now. And how 'bout you? Would you like to join Gavin and me for dinner? He's made a big pot of chili."

That was an invitation I couldn't resist. "That sure beats the bowl of popcorn I was thinking of eating. Let me run Wendy home, and I'll be right there."

When she heard Wendy was with me, Libby insisted I bring her and Belle too, and it was a done deal. I dropped Wendy off at Sunshine Cottage. Belle was probably dressed in what she dubbed her housedress and would want to change clothes, so I backtracked to the Olde Mill Inn on my own.

Paddington was washing his face and studying Raggedy Anne and Andy. I knew he was thinking the long red and white striped scarves looked inviting. "You know better, don't you?"

"Not you too, Leta. All I hear all day is 'Don't you dare. That's not a cat toy.' Why not, I ask you?"

Rolling him over for a belly rub, I smiled at him. "Silly boy. Now, tell me, have you seen Dickens and Buttercup? You know they're missing, don't you?"

"I heard Libby and Jill talking about it, but I haven't seen them. I saw Watson, though. He was hightailing it up the path to the pub. Snooty thing, he didn't even stop to talk."

"When was that?"

"Just before dark yesterday. He's probably back at the manor house now."

I wanted to think he was following the dogs, but it didn't seem very likely. "Well, Paddington, can you keep a lookout for Dickens and Buttercup, please? Someone thinks they saw Dickens near the bridge this morning."

"I can do that. I'll head that way. It could be that some of my friends have seen them."

Once again, an image from *101 Dalmations* came to mind—the scene where the dogs across the land bark an alert about the missing puppies. I smiled as I imagined cats, dogs, and foxes providing updates to Paddington. *Whatever it takes.*

Opening the front door, I called hello and walked to the kitchen. It was a repeat of the scene from the other day, except Libby was at the table while Gavin stirred the big pot of chili. A timer pinged as I entered, and Gavin opened the oven door to pull out two loaves of bread.

"Do you need a taster? I'm at your service."

"No tastes until after appetizers," Libby said. "Jill made a batch of sausage balls, so we'll start with those."

The inn was often empty or sparsely populated on Tuesdays and Wednesdays, and tonight, only one room was booked. Those guests were in Chipping Camden having dinner at Michael's Mediterranean, one of my favorite restaurants.

Gavin turned the flame beneath the chili to low and suggested Libby and I retire to the sitting room. He soon followed with the sausage balls and a bottle of red wine. Choosing the chair closest to the fireplace, I tucked my feet under me and accepted the glass he poured me.

It wasn't long before we heard Wendy coming in the front door. She explained that Belle was still at the manor house. "Imagine my surprise to find only Tigger waiting for me when I got home. That's when I saw the note saying that Ellie had invited Mum to spend the day on the Canine Caper, as they're calling it, and go to Broadway for dinner out."

As I sipped wine, she answered questions about what we'd done in Bourton and Stow to get the word out about the dogs. Libby and Gavin were hearing much of this for the first time and were horrified by the dognapping story.

"Well, the good news," said Wendy, "is that if Dickens was spotted on the road, then he wasn't *napped*. Is that even a word?"

Gavin smiled. "It's not funny, but I'm picturing Buttercup leading Dickens astray. That dog likes to wander. I bet she took off, and your little hero dog ran after her to bring her back. He knows better than to run away."

Wendy agreed. "Dickens lives the life of Riley, and there's no way he'd ever leave Leta. He's smarter than that."

I felt myself relaxing for the first time that day, and I was in danger of dozing off. Gavin's next comment told me I was right. "Why don't we serve dinner in the kitchen, before Leta starts snoring?"

Libby and Gavin had dinner on the table in no time. She pulled out bowls of sour cream and grated cheddar cheese to serve with the chili while Gavin sliced and buttered the fresh-baked whole grain bread. It was a dinner of simple fare that hit the spot.

Seconds were being offered and declined when Gemma arrived. After giving Libby a peck on the cheek, she turned to me. "Any word about Dickens?"

This was typical Gemma behavior. She could be insensitive one moment and caring the next, though more often, her curt, nearly rude, persona won out. When I hesitated, Wendy stepped in to bring her up to speed.

Gemma propped her hip against the counter. "That's encouraging. Hopefully, you'll soon get a call that he's turned up in someone's garden, maybe with Buttercup in tow."

When she was seated with a bowl of chili, she told us that the news of the hour was the weather. "They're mentioning snow, but as is typical, exactly when and how much shifts by the hour. We don't often get snow in December, so I'm not holding my breath."

Her comment made me think of Atlanta snowstorms. "It's the same for Atlanta. I recall one year it snowed on Christmas—not much, but enough to be pretty. Our worst storms come in January, February, and March. Goodness, I remember one year when I was teaching a leadership program at a resort south of the city. It was March, and we had to end early so folks could get home before it hit. We went from enjoying the azaleas to the city shutting down with four inches of snow."

Gavin drummed his fingers on the table. "Hmm. I think that's around 25 centimeters. We wouldn't know what to do if we got that much snow. What's the prediction, Gemma?"

"Oh, anywhere from 5 to 10 centimeters. If it's only 5 centimeters, it will be pretty, but not much of a problem. Much more than that and things will get dicey. Not many drivers have snow tires."

I groaned. "I don't, so I guess I should head to Waitrose tomorrow. You know I was visiting my sister in Atlanta last year when Astonbury got snow, so I missed it."

"Leta," Libby said, "Wednesday is Gavin's day to do the shopping at the Co-op. We have to prepare for our weekend guests, even if they all end up canceling. If you text him a list tonight or first thing in the morning, he can pick up a few things for you."

"Dad, if you go tomorrow, you should miss the panic buying because the latest forecast is for it to hit Friday or Saturday."

As the conversation moved to the various holiday celebrations that could be impacted by the weather, my thoughts shifted to Dickens and Buttercup in the snow. *I have to find them.*

CHAPTER NINE

WEDNESDAY MORNING, AS I poured Christie's milk and my coffee—in that order—I heard meowing outside the kitchen door. I opened the door expecting to see Watson, but it was Paddington.

The handsome Burmese cat peered into the kitchen as though he wasn't sure about coming in. Christie picked up on his hesitation. "Oh, come in here. I won't hurt you."

I stifled a laugh. Paddington had avoided Christie ever since her first visit to the inn, when she'd all but run him out of the conservatory. Though he played with Dickens, he tended to keep his distance from Christie. And he rarely visited us.

Picking him up, I stroked his head. "Is Watson out there too?"

"Nope, just me. I haven't seen Watson in a few days now."

That's odd. "Well then, what brings you here, young man?"

"Punky saw a white dog in Bourton. He was drinking from the river, and she thinks there was another dog curled up by the back door of one of the restaurants. She saw a cat too, but that's nothing new."

Christie's ears stood on high alert. "Is Punky a cat?"

"Yes, and she's much friendlier than you."

Feline personalities weren't my main interest. "When did Punky see the dogs, Paddington? Was it last night or the night before?" I thought someone would have noticed and reported two stray dogs in Bourton if it were during the day.

He licked his paw before replying. "It was the middle of the night when I saw her, and she was on her way home. She'd just seen them. Punky especially likes the fish and chips restaurant in Bourton. She says their garbage cans are the best."

This was good news and bad. This meant they for sure hadn't fallen prey to dognappers. But putting this new information together with what I'd heard from the woman who called yesterday told me the two were traveling farther afield. *Where on earth are they going?*

The cat conversation shifted to food and why their pet parents didn't provide table scraps. Sipping my coffee, I stared out the window. There had to be something I could do to locate the wanderers—something beyond hoping someone would call to say the two were safe and sound.

A phone call interrupted my thoughts. It was a new experience for me to be anxious when an unknown number appeared on my cell phone. Instead of a robocall, it could be news about the dogs—but would it be good news or bad?

This caller was from Little Rissington and had also sighted the dogs. He said they were near the tree line on his property before dawn and wouldn't come near the door. "I took them a bowl of water and some of my Frankie's kibble. They stood back and watched, as though they needed to be sure the coast was clear before they approached the food. They must have been starving because when I l closed my door and looked out the window, the food was gone and so were they."

"You don't know how thankful I am to hear from you. At least I know they're okay."

"It was only by chance that I picked up your flyer in Bourton yesterday. You live in Astonbury. Is that right?"

"Yes, and I have no idea why they bolted from my driveway or why they haven't come back."

As I explained the circumstances to him, he seemed as puzzled as I was. "That means they've traveled a good distance since they left. Well, I hope you get them back before it snows—if it does. The forecast is wrong as often as it's right, you know."

I thanked him and started the grocery list I'd promised to send Gavin. The call had reminded me that I needed to stock up. Surveying the pantry and the fridge made me realize I needed more than I thought, so I texted Gavin that I would make the grocery run for myself. At least shopping would be a distraction from my worry about the dogs. And cooking. I pulled out my recipe box in search of casseroles and soups I could make over the coming days—things that would freeze well.

Bolognese sauce would work for several meals—simple pasta with sauce plus a batch or two of baked ziti. I hadn't made chicken corn chowder or vegetable soup in a while, and those recipes each made enough to feed an army. If I planned well, I would have several meals for the next week and a freezer full of easy dinners when Dave arrived for Christmas.

The list was nearly finished when the phone rang, and Posh Pets appeared on the screen. "Hello, Mindy."

"Sorry, not Mindy. This is Ric. I've got some good news, I think. When we took your flyers to Pepper's last night, one of the volunteers thought he'd seen the dogs on Monday night."

"On the way to Bourton?"

"Um, no. The other direction. He lives in Clapton-on-the-Hill and saw them there, trotting along the road coming toward Northleach. What made you think it was Bourton?"

When I told him about my other two callers, he wondered if the Clapton-on-the-Hill sighting was a mistake. "I'll wager he saw two dogs and mistook them for yours, since they were top of mind. It was from a distance, and he did mention one was a blotchy brown and white and wondered whether Dickens had been rolling in the dirt."

"What do you think, Ric? You have more experience with stray dogs than I do."

"I'd say, based on what you've told me, that the Clapton pair weren't Dickens and Buttercup. But that's good news that they've been spotted twice near Bourton." Little did he know they'd been spotted three times—if you counted Punky.

"I wish I knew what was going on in their doggie brains. It's like they're off on some big adventure."

"It's hard to say, Leta. You're not in this category, but I get so angry with our weekenders and summer visitors who are careless with their animals. The poor dogs are down from London or some other big city and get anxious when left to their own devices. Their owners go off for a day trip, leave them in the garden, and the dog thinks it's been left behind. At least, that's what I imagine happens when the animal breaks out of the garden and is found wandering."

"Do they usually get reunited with their owners?"

"Most of the time, but it can take a while because the information on the tag gives a London address or home number. If it's a cell phone, that makes it easier."

"I thought it was a requirement that all pets be chipped."

"Yes, but even with that, the information can be out of date. Anyway, that doesn't explain what's up with your two. Look, one of the things I try to do when I'm at the shelter is to compare missing dog posts with the strays that come in, but if yours are as far away as Little Rissington, they won't be brought in here. When I go in tonight, I'll fax your flyer to the shelters over that way so they can be on the lookout too."

He said he'd let me know if he heard anything else and wished me well. *Such a nice young man.*

By early afternoon, I had unloaded groceries and was ready to start a pot of Bolognese sauce. I often changed up recipes, and this time I was mixing ground pork with the ground beef. It was pretty hard to mess up a good sauce if you knew the basics.

A knock on the door interrupted me as I was pulling out pots and utensils. I was surprised to see that it was Sarah. "Hi, Leta. I'm on my way to Stow and just hung up with Lucy. I didn't plan to tell her about the dogs, but when she asked about Buttercup, I couldn't avoid the subject. She wanted me to be sure to tell you it's not my fault or yours. Buttercup stayed close to home when Lucy and her sister lived together, but since her bout with old dog disease, she wanders a bit more. ”

"That's kind of her, but I still feel responsible. Did you tell her we're doing everything we can to locate the two?"

"Yes, I assured her you had gone above and beyond. She feels bad that Buttercup involved Dickens in her escapade, as she put it."

Sarah was encouraged by the news of the various sightings and expressed her confidence that the wanderers would soon return. "Your work is paying off, Leta. Now, it's off to Stow for me."

And it's back to cooking for me. With my favorite Christmas CDs playing, I chopped onions and garlic and browned the meat. I hummed along to my favorite Perry Como song, "C-H-R-I-S-T-M-A-S," and recalled taking the album to show and tell in grade school. I'd never heard anyone else sing the song that explained what each letter in Christmas stood for. *Isn't it funny the things that stay with you?*

The music shifted to Frank Sinatra singing "Have Yourself a Merry Little Christmas," and I thought of my mother playing the same collections when I was a child—Bing Crosby, Johnny Mathis, and Dean Martin. And the Chipmunk song! That was one I didn't have on CD.

"Christie, I need elves to help me decorate the trees, or at least the big one in the sitting room. I wonder whether I can get Belle, Ellie, Wendy, and Peter to come over tonight?" That was a silly question. I'd never known them to turn down a dinner invitation, even if it was last minute.

As I dialed Ellie, I pictured a pan of baked ziti and a Greek salad. Maybe I could get Wendy to bring dessert. Ellie agreed right away, and I realized the two senior members of the LOLs were together when I heard her say, "Belle, what do you think about dinner at Leta's tonight?"

I heard unintelligible murmurs before Ellie came back to me. "Leta, Belle says that would be perfect, and we can bring you up-to-date on the Canine Caper investigation too. She brought the police reports over this morning, and we've made great progress comparing them to what we learned from the lost dog posts on the *Astonbury Aha*."

"Super. I'll text Peter and Wendy, and I'll ask Wendy to pick up dessert at Toby's."

Ellie had a better idea. "Caroline baked cookies today. Why don't I bring a tin of those?"

That was an offer I couldn't refuse. Caroline was an excellent cook and baker. When I texted Peter and Wendy, they both accepted the invitation, and Wendy said she'd bring two bottles of red wine.

Stirring the sauce, I turned the heat to low and pulled out the whole-milk mozzarella and block of Parmesan cheese. It was a rare occasion when I took the shortcut of buying already shredded or grated cheese. The flavor just couldn't compare. I thinly sliced the soft mozzarella and then grated the Parmesan.

I positioned two rectangular casserole dishes next to the cheeses and the pot and snapped a photo to text to Dave with the words, "Guess what's for dinner?"

The phone rang immediately. "If I guess right, will you save me some? Is it baked ziti?"

"Good guess, and I'm way ahead of you. I'm making two pans, one for tonight and one to freeze. We're decorating the trees tonight."

"I wish I could be there for the tree trimming, but I will be next year. I almost hate to ask, but tell me the latest on Dickens. You haven't texted anything since early this morning."

"No updates. Given that both sightings have been predawn, I have the sense they sleep at night and get an early start. But why?"

"You'll have to ask Dickens when he comes home. You know he will, don't you?"

I had to believe he was right. "You better believe
I'll be asking Dickens to explain himself. Right
before I ground him for life."

"That's my girl. Say hi to the gang for me and call
me before you turn out the light. Love you."

The first guest to arrive was Ellie. Setting the
cookies on the counter, she said she'd be right back
and returned with a flipchart pad.

"Oh my goodness, you ladies were serious about
a report, weren't you?"

"You set us a task, dear. Of course, we're serious.
And I think we've done amazing work, if I do say
so myself."

I ushered her to the sitting room and lit the
candles on the mantel. The table was already set
with the new holiday runner I'd purchased at the
tree lighting, and spinach dip with crackers sat on
a tray ready to be carried to the large ottoman.

When the Davies family arrived, Peter escorted
his mum to the comfortable chair by the fire and

Wendy uncorked the wine. I popped the baked ziti in the oven and joined my friends in the sitting room, where Peter had already pulled out the Christmas lights. Together, we wrapped them around the tree. Putting lights on a tree was much easier with two people.

Wendy clapped her hands. "A marvelous start. Let's do your mom's Woolworth's ornaments next."

As Belle handed the delicate glass ornaments to Peter and Wendy, Ellie opened the box labeled *White House ornaments*. "I heard about these. George Evans was quite taken with them at your party last year."

Christie jumped into Belle's lap and purred, "Where's the black and white cat with the Santa hat?"

That reminded me I hadn't unpacked my collection of stuffed animals. They were my pride and joy—teddy bears, cats, a floppy moose, and a mouse or two. Smiling, I sat on the floor and pulled them from a large box.

When the buzzer went off for the baked ziti, I pulled it from the oven, popped a loaf of Italian bread in its place, and threw together the salad.

No one mentioned Dickens until we began to clear the table. As we sent the ladies to the sitting room, Peter scraped the dishes and stacked them on the counter while I filled the sink with hot soapy water. I added the last dish to the water and looked at him. "It doesn't seem right that Dickens isn't here to lick a plate or two."

He squeezed my shoulder. "He'll be back, Leta. I know he will."

The sitting room decorated in greens and reds was always cozy, but when the Christmas tree and holiday trimmings came out, it was my favorite room. As the final touch before we got down to business, I handed Peter the delicate crocheted angel to place on top of the tree.

Ellie stood and stuck the large Post-it pages to the window overlooking the garden. She beamed as she gazed around the room. "Listen my children, and you shall hear . . . " There was a smile in her voice as well as on her face. "No, it's not Paul Revere, but it's an intriguing story."

When she pulled out a laser pointer, Peter choked on his wine. "Ellie, where on earth did you get that?"

"At the office supply shop, of course."

She waited for us to stop laughing before she proceeded. "Belle and I were very methodical. First, we reviewed the missing dog posts on the *Astonbury Aha* going back sixty days and captured dates, locations, owners, and dogs. Then, we studied the police reports and outlined the same information. There were some duplicates, but not that many. In other words, some owners posted on the *Astonbury Aha and* reported their missing dogs to the police, but most did only one or the other."

Raising her hand, Belle interjected, "Let me clarify. Not many villages have an online news source like Astonbury does, so in those places—Stroud is one—the owners went to the police station. Here and in neighboring villages, the dog owners more often posted the alert on the *Astonbury Aha* and didn't bother with the police."

Ellie pointed to two pages, one on top of the other, stuck horizontally to the window. It was a spreadsheet with five columns—Dog, Where, Date Missing, Police, and Online. The rows were numbered down the left side. "See here? The first twenty-odd dogs all come from the police reports you gave us. We have the dates they went missing, a checkmark in the police column, and another checkmark under Online if the information was posted there too."

Christie had been watching the red dot emitted by the laser pointer. She was chirping. That was the only way I could describe the sound, the same one she made when she watched the birds at the feeder. I knew she would make a move soon.

Wendy studied the chart. "So, most of these, mainly from beyond our area, were only reported to the police. Stroud, Lower Slaughter, Stanway, and Evesham. Only a few were posted online as well."

Pursing my lips, I took in the names. "I see. Those last several include Bingo, whose owner called me. And then there's Tank, who belongs to Jonas's sister, and Dickens and Buttercup as a single listing. So in a handful of cases, the owners covered both bases—the police and online."

"Right, now look at the next chart." She drew our attention with the laser pointer.

And that's when Christie pounced. She did her little butt wiggle before leaping up the wall in a frenzied attempt to catch the red dot. After the third leap, she looked at me and meowed. "Why won't it stop? I want it."

As we laughed at my frustrated cat, Ellie playfully tapped her foot. "Shall we continue?"

She explained the layout of the data. "We started with the pet owners who went to the police. At the top are the owners in Stroud and Lower Slaughter who reported their missing dogs to the police *and* later got phone calls—not a note, like Bob Weir did. These were ransom demands over the phone."

Wendy glanced my way. "Leta, Constable James was right. Dognappers do exist here. Did the owners pay?"

Nodding, Ellie frowned. "Yes. Belle and I discovered that because we contacted them. It wasn't noted on the police report. The owners said they didn't want to tell the police about the ransom demands. They were afraid the police would either tell them not to pay it or would get involved in some way that would ruin their chances of getting the family pet back."

Peter shook his head. "Just like on the telly—a ransom exchange gone bad."

"But wait," I said, "Jonas explained to me that the police *don't* get involved. That's the problem. They treat it like a property crime. Didn't the officers at the other stations explain that to the owners?"

Ellie frowned. "The best I can tell, Leta, they didn't. Just made noises about not having the manpower to investigate but would be on the alert if any information came to their attention."

Using her pointer, she directed us back to the page on the wall. "We learned that one dog was a Staffordshire bull terrier, one was a Jack Russell, and the third was a scruffy mixed breed. That owner commented that his dog might not be special to anyone else, but he was willing to pay whatever it took to get him back. He paid two hundred pounds!"

I would pay that and more to get Dickens back. "How did they pay and get their dogs? I mean, was it a ransom drop like we see in the movies?"

"All three followed the instructions to leave the money in a can beneath the Stanway cricket pavilion and then drive to the Stanway Church and wait. There had to be two dognappers working together because almost as soon as the owner parked at the church, they received a text saying the dog was tied to a post on the Cotswolds Way near the pavilion. I imagine one person waited near the church to be sure the owner was there, and the other fetched and counted the money when the coast was clear and then tied the dog to the post."

I pictured Dickens tied to a post, patiently waiting for me to rescue him. "Maybe I'm being overly optimistic, but I have to believe Dickens and Buttercup are off on some grand adventure, and they haven't been dognapped."

Peter put another log on the fire. "I agree with you, Leta. I think you would have had a ransom demand by now if someone had them. And if the caller from Little Rissington is right about what he saw, they're fine—hungry maybe, but fine. So, the good news is these other pet owners got their dogs back safe and sound. The bad news is Ellie found at least three cases of dognapping. I wonder whether there are more."

Ellie shook her head. "Not that we know of. The strange thing I learned when I googled the subject is that there are more dognappings in West Yorkshire than there are in London—not that there aren't plenty in the city. Now, let's talk about these last few."

Wendy held up her hand. "Wait, before you get to those, what do you plan to do with the information you collected on the ransom cases? It seems to me that the police need to know about this pattern."

"We're a step ahead of you. Belle and I have already written up a report to give to Constable James. Even if the police are short on manpower now, it may be something he can pursue. What if these thieves are involved in other crimes? What if they escalate?"

With a wave of her hand, she steered the conversation to the remaining cases. "The owners live in Astonbury, Northleach, and Bourton-on-the-Water. All posted their missing dogs online, but only Bob Weir reported his dog to the police. We made an executive decision that we would contact the other owners who posted their missing dog information online. We didn't need to check with you, Leta, or Bob Weir, or Jonas."

It was a serious subject, but the dowager countess was enjoying herself. One more sheet of paper was stuck to the window, but it had been folded and taped so its contents were hidden. She tugged on it to reveal a colorful chart.

They must have choreographed this because Belle rose to her feet and took the pointer from Ellie. She had our full attention as well as Christie's. "These conversations were quite revealing." She pointed to the third row on the page. The black writing was struck through in red and someone had drawn a devil's face beneath it. "This man did not get his dog back. Do you know why? Because when Pepper's Animal Shelter called him in London to say they had his poor pup at the shelter, he said he didn't want him back, that he was too much trouble. Can you imagine? If there were a list somewhere of people who should never be allowed to have pets, his name would be on it."

Peter grumbled. "There's a special place in hell for people like him."

"The good news is all but one of the dogs is back with its owner, and the one that's still missing may yet be returned." She pointed to a row with an asterisk. "I'll tell you more about that one in a moment."

She twirled the pointer around two names. "These two received phone calls from villagers who had seen their dog wandering and picked the animal up and put it in their garage or their walled garden." She moved the pointer to another name. "This one got a call from Pepper's Animal Shelter when the dog was turned in. Those chips are a wonderful thing."

I leaned forward. "What was different about the others? They got their dogs back too, right?"

Her eyes twinkled. "This is where it gets interesting. These owners found notes just like your Mr. Weir—with cut-out letters. None were threatening, but they all had cryptic messages and had long since been thrown away. For that reason, the recipients couldn't remember the exact message, just the gist of it. Oh, and usually, they found the envelopes on the floor in the morning, as though someone crept up and put them through the letterbox at night."

Ellie read from a sheet of paper. "Do you miss your dog? Where is your dog? Take care of your dog. Things like that. And then a day later, sometimes two, someone called to say they'd found the dog, and subsequently returned it. Everyone was happy. In all these cases, the dog was no worse for the wear. In fact, the rescuers either bathed or brushed the dog, and the owners were delighted."

Returning to her chair, Belle cleared her throat. "Because Bob Weir told Leta that he'd given Bingo's rescuer a reward, Ellie asked the other owners if they had done that."

"Oh! I'm sorry. I forgot to mention that Jonas's sister gave some money to the young girl who returned Tank." I looked at Ellie. "What was the answer? Did they all give a reward or tip to the person who brought their dog back?"

Ellie's smile told me I was right. She explained that in each case, the owner had handsomely rewarded the person who returned their pet. In true detective fashion, she asked lots of good questions. What did the person look like? What kind of car did they drive? How were they dressed?

"Tank was returned by a young soft-spoken girl, according to Jonas's sister. Her four-year-old remembered that she wore a T-shirt with a cat on it. She didn't want to accept the money and tried to leave without it. His sister said she all but stuffed it in the girl's pocket until finally, she took it. The physical description was vague, only that she was slim and medium height."

I frowned. "That could describe me—even the cat T-shirt."

Wendy laughed. "You may be taller than I am, but most people would still call you short."

Belle smiled at us. "You two! Anyway, that was the only time it was a girl. The others were brought back by a young man." She chuckled. "Have you ever noticed that the older we get, pretty much anyone from school age to their midthirties is called a young man or woman? For me, it may be anyone younger than fifty."

Wendy's mouth dropped open. "You're right. It's hard for me to tell anymore whether someone's in their twenties or thirties unless their clothes give them away. Even that's not a reliable indicator these days."

Peter held up his hand. "Okay, we're getting sidetracked. Were the other dogs returned by a man—young or otherwise?"

Ellie nodded. "A young man, they all said. I think the owners are so happy to get their pets back that they pay very little attention to the person who comes to the door. In this case, the description was just as vague. A young man, perhaps dressed in a dark hoodie, wearing a nondescript ball cap that covered his hair. Maybe tall, maybe very tall. He also politely declined the money but wound up taking it in the end—every time."

"Car?" Peter asked.

"No car was seen. The chihuahua owner thinks it was someone on a bicycle with the dog in a pouch on the handlebars. Like the book we read for book club in September, *Nala's World*, where the cat rides in a red pouch. The other two times, the car must have been parked down the lane."

Christie leaped into Belle's lap and meowed loudly. "Never mind that silly cat on the bicycle. Where's Watson?"

"Shh," Belle said as she stroked her. "I'm here now."

I chuckled at their interaction and posed Christie's question. "Ellie, Nala makes me think of Watson. He doesn't ride on a bike, but he usually visits here daily, often twice a day. Except I haven't seen him at all yesterday or today. Is he sticking close to the manor house?"

Her answer surprised me. "Come to think of it, I haven't seen him either. I wonder if he pestered Caroline before I made it to the kitchen for my morning tea. I'll ask her."

Peter looked at his mother. "Mum, tell us about the dog that's still missing."

The corners of Belle's mouth lifted. "Panda—isn't that a cute name? She's a fluffy black and white mutt, and she disappeared from the garden last night when her owner put her out just before bedtime. Mrs. Miller is quite distraught, and she posted a notice on the *Astonbury Aha* first thing this morning."

Ellie picked up the story. "And now, as they say, the plot thickens."

Uh-oh. Why do I think they're up to something?

"Belle and I have put a plan in action. Mrs. Miller will keep us posted about any messages. In fact, I expect a call any moment because she promised to call before she retired for the evening. We're pretty sure she won't have received an envelope in her letterbox yet. Those seem to show up in the morning. Perhaps she'll get a phone call. We don't know."

Looking quite pleased with themselves, Belle and Ellie glanced at each other. Wendy, Peter, and I wore concerned expressions.

Ellie placed her wine glass on the side table. "Once she calls, we plan to stake out her cottage to see whether anyone delivers a note."

I almost choked. "You what? A stakeout?"

Wendy blurted what I was thinking. "Mum, have you lost your mind? And you talk about me and Leta taking risks."

"Tsk, tsk," Belle said. "We'll be in a car with the lights off. It's not as if someone's going to creep up on us and break a window."

"Mum," Wendy said. "It will be dark. What can you possibly see from the car?" She blanched. "Oh for goodness' sake, I can't believe I said that. Surely you don't plan to leave the car, do you?"

Ellie chuckled. "We won't leave the car because we have to follow them."

When I heard that, I gasped. "Follow them! And then what?"

I could tell Peter had heard enough when he stood. "Okay, Mum. That's it. I want to say I forbid it—like you used to say to me—but I know I can't do that. If you're serious about this, I'm going with you."

Has the whole world gone mad?

Peter wasn't a member of the Little Old Ladies' Detective Agency, but he took charge. First, he pointed out that the messenger could appear any time between bedtime and dawn. "Do you two plan to stay there all night?"

Ellie drew a deep breath and explained that indeed they did. They would take turns napping, and if no one showed up by dawn, they'd go home and try again Thursday night. "Peter, I'll admit the part I'm concerned about is following someone without my lights on. That's the way they do it on the telly. But there is a full moon tonight, so we should be fine."

I was trying to figure out how to forestall their plan when Wendy offered a compromise. "Peter, you're the only one of us who has a business to run. You can't stay out all night. Here's another idea. Why not let Ellie and Leta take the early shift, and Mum and I take over at two a.m.? That way, we all get some sleep."

Grumbling, Peter stood. "Great, now all four of you can put yourselves in danger. How is that a better idea?"

Belle gave her son a stern look. "Peter, leave it be. I appreciate your concern, but we'll be careful."

Ellie's phone ringing prevented Peter from responding. It was Mrs. Miller saying she was going to bed and had received neither a note nor a call. She would leave the light on over her front door.

That was all Belle needed to hear. "Peter, that's your cue to take me and your sister home. Wendy will set the alarm, and we'll relieve Leta and Ellie at two if we don't hear from them any earlier."

None of this seemed like a good idea to me, but I was outnumbered. It was typical of Wendy to come up with a risky idea, but this was new behavior for Belle and Ellie. *A stakeout, for goodness' sake.*

CHAPTER TEN

ELLIE CONTINUED TO SURPRISE me. While I was changing into warm clothes—black, of course—she brought a similar ensemble inside. I couldn't help laughing when she called it her *stakeout* outfit, and wouldn't have been surprised if she'd pulled out black face paint to daub on her cheeks and nose.

On the way, I texted Dave that I was on an adventure with Ellie. He was curious but not worried. If I'd mentioned Wendy, on the other hand, he would have called immediately. Between the two of us, she was hands down the bigger risk-taker.

I knew Ellie had thought it through when she backed into a driveway a few doors down from Mrs. Miller's home. "Mrs. Miller said this cottage was a rental and unoccupied until Friday. This way, Leta, we can pull out in an instant."

We started our watch talking of holiday plans and the book club selection for the next night and then spent the next several hours in companionable silence with one or the other of us occasionally voicing a random thought.

"Did you read the book *Pepper's Pies* when you were a child, Leta?"

"I don't think so. I read *The Five Little Peppers*. Is it about the same family?"

"No. I thought of it when you mentioned Polly and Ric volunteering at Pepper's Animal Shelter. It opened in the '80s when the author left a sizable sum to build a shelter on her property in Northleach, with the royalties from *Pepper's Pies* going to the shelter in perpetuity to fund it long term. Her grandson, who owned a farm and was forever taking in strays, was her only beneficiary, and he put his heart and soul into carrying out her wishes. I understand the royalties are starting to dry up for some reason, and the shelter is in dire straits."

"Did the book have something to do with animals?"

Though I couldn't see Ellie's face in the dark car, I detected a smile in her voice. "Oh yes. It was a beloved children's book in the '50s. Perhaps it never made it to America. Pepper is a lad who loves dogs *and* sweets. One day he sees a dog dig a hole beneath the garden gate and trot down the street. When he chases the little thing and brings it home to its owner, she rewards him with a piece of cherry pie. Soon after, he finds another dog on the loose and returns it, and once again, the reward is a slice of pie."

I chuckled. "It sounds like a story I would have enjoyed, but it doesn't ring a bell."

"My sons and grandsons loved the book. Pepper gets the idea to unlatch one garden gate a day, pick up a dog, and deliver it to the owner's front door. One day he gets greedy and opens gates and returns dogs up and down the street until he gets a tummy ache. The illustrations are priceless—a lad with his mouth covered with fruit pie, rubbing his swollen tummy. On the next page, the buttons have popped off his shirt. And by the end, he's in bed with a thermometer in his mouth.

"When the neighbors hear he's ill, they line up outside the door with their dogs and their pies, and that's when they realize what he's been up to. It was meant to be a humorous lesson about the sin of gluttony, but Nicholas and Matthew loved it for the dogs. And there you have it, the story of how

Pepper's Animal Shelter came to be. If it survives until next year, maybe we should choose it as the charity to support with the proceeds from the Fall Fête. In the meantime, I think I'll send a donation."

"Ric mentioned they were struggling, but I had no idea it was in danger of closing. I think I'll do the same."

Beyond our intermittent chatter, it was a quiet night, and my eyes were half-closed when I saw the gleam of headlights. It was Wendy and Belle, ready to relieve us. When Ellie cranked her car and pulled out, Wendy took our place and doused her lights.

"Ellie, how likely do you think it is that Mrs. Miller is a target?"

"Oh, I haven't calculated the odds, Leta. Belle and I simply thought it was too good an opportunity to pass up. I *do* think, however, that whoever is delivering these notes is more likely to show up earlier in the night, so I don't expect Wendy and

Belle will have any luck on their shift. We'll give it another try tomorrow night."

I was dead to the world when my phone rang the next morning. As I reached for it, I squinted at the alarm clock—seven thirty. *Has someone found the dogs?*

A loud, gruff voice thundered down the line. "Leta Parker! How dare you! First the station in Stow and now the ones in Stroud and Evesham."

It took me a moment to come fully awake and recognize the voice, but I should have known immediately. Detective Chief Inspector Brian Burton was the only person who ever spoke to me this way. "What? What are you talking about?"

"You know full well. It wasn't enough that you talked Constable James into helping you? You had to involve my officers from two other stations?"

He was the only person who never failed to goad me into raising my voice. "What? I haven't spoken with anyone except Constable James." I was about to say, "And he called me," but there was no reason to throw Jonas under the bus.

"Don't play dumb with me. You may not have picked up the phone yourself, but I know that when Mrs. Davies and the dowager countess ring my police stations, you're the one behind it."

Did they tell me they did that? I can't remember. But why does it matter?

It's difficult to get huffy when you're lying in bed in a flannel nightgown, but I did my best. "Now, you wait a minute. I don't know what you're talking about, but it's not a crime to ask the police for help, is it?"

"As a matter of fact, it is! I could charge those two with 'causing wasteful employment of the police,' which is a criminal offense. They should count themselves lucky that I don't hold them responsible for their actions—because I know you put them up to it."

"Oh, for goodness' sake. Here I am worried sick about Dickens and his new friend Buttercup, and you called to yell at me? To accuse me of breaking the law?"

"I did, and that's not the only law you've broken. From what I hear, your dog is running loose at this very moment because you failed to keep him under control. Has he or has he not been spotted on the road without being on a lead? That, Mrs. Parker, is also a criminal offense."

"Excuse me? You think I wouldn't have him by my side if I had a choice? He ran off, something he's never done before, and I'm doing everything I can to find him." I tried to stop spluttering. "Does every dog owner whose dog runs off get a phone call like this?"

He hesitated. "Only the worst offenders. And this dog business has gotten out of hand. Consider yourself warned. If you waste police time on this matter again, I *will* charge you."

I was about to hang up on him, but he beat me to it. *The nerve of the man.*

Christie leaped to the bed and stood on my chest. "We slept late. I'm hungry."

If I was looking for sympathy, I was in the wrong place. I threw the covers off, rolled to my side, and stuck my feet into my red wool slippers.

Christie escorted me to the bathroom, talking all the way. "Hurry. I'm starving."

She twined around my ankles as I splashed cold water on my face and studied my reflection. It was not a pretty sight. The deep crease on one cheek and the dark circles beneath my brown eyes told me I had slept hard—not long enough, but hard. Tying the sash around my red fleece robe, I followed Christie downstairs.

Thank goodness I operated on autopilot most mornings. Hit the button for the coffee, pull milk from the fridge for Christie, let Dickens out, and toss him a treat—except there was no Dickens. I poured a cup of coffee and sat at the kitchen table with my chin in my hands.

"Christie, maybe I should drive to Little Rissington and tour the village lanes. Would Dickens come running if he saw my car? Is he lost? I don't understand why he hasn't gone up to someone's front door for food. It's not like him to miss a meal."

My rambling must have worried Christie because she jumped to my lap and patted my cheek with her paw. "Leta, maybe it's something about Buttercup. Maybe she's scared of new people."

"I don't know, Christie. I'm beginning to wonder whether the people who've called really saw Dickens. It could have been any white dog. Why would he stay away for so long? Why did he leave in the first place?"

My spiraling thoughts were interrupted by a call from Ellie wanting to know if I'd had any news about Dickens. "No, but I did have a rude wake-up call from our favorite DCI, which reminds me, I need to call Gemma. Can you believe the man told me I'd broken the law in more than one way?"

When I shared the accusations he'd made, Ellie jumped in. "That man is rude beyond belief and has no business dealing with the public, nor being in charge of a police force. Don't spend any time worrying about him. I'll ring Andrew Lytton as soon as we hang up, and he'll handle this situation should anything come of it."

Andrew Lytton was the solicitor Ellie had arranged for me when the police in Torquay took me in. It was comforting to know I could rely on him if DCI Burton made good on his threats to charge me.

"Now, Leta, I have a suggestion about tonight's stakeout."

I groaned. "Oh Ellie, I haven't had enough coffee to tackle that topic."

"All you have to do is listen. Peter rang me first thing to tell me he's not happy about Wendy and his mother being out together playing Agatha Raisin and Miss Marple, as he puts it. So, the two of us agreed that he and Belle would take the first watch tonight. Mrs. Miller will spend the night with her sister in Cheltenham, so Peter and Belle will be in place by 6:00 unless we hear that Mrs. Miller got a call or a note before then. She'll leave the outside light on for us when she leaves around 6:30. After book club, you, Wendy, and I will take over. It will be a long night for the three of us, but I'll drive the Bentley, so we'll be very comfortable. We can take turns napping."

How can I say no to an offer like that? "Okay, I guess. Since I'm the one who asked you to look into missing dogs, I can hardly refuse."

"Of course you can't. You put us in charge of the Canine Caper, and we intend to solve it."

That left me to work on the "Disappearance of Dickens." Topping off my mug of coffee, I carried it to the sitting room and started the fire. It was a grey, dreary day, almost as though the sky was readying itself for the snow predicted to arrive at some point in the next few days.

Desperate to come up with something else I could do to find them, I tried Google. Sure enough, there was tons of information on why dogs run away, how far they go, and more. Labrador retrievers were number one on the list of dogs most likely to run away, but golden retrievers weren't mentioned; nor were Great Pyrenees like Dickens. Another site placed Labs on a list of dogs least likely to run away. So which was it—most likely or least likely? Who knew?

It was heartening to read that dogs could pick up scents from as far away as ten miles in the right conditions, meaning they could find their way home—if they wanted to. *Surely, Dickens wants to!* On the other hand, it was *disheartening* to read that big strong dogs could run five miles in a day—some might travel as far as fourteen miles. Dickens and Buttercup were both relatively large, but Buttercup was elderly, and I wondered if that might slow the adventurers down.

The other good news was the fact that a dog's instinct to find food and water will take over, which would explain the two staying near villages. The bad news was that a lost dog could likely survive months or even years on its own. Of course, I wanted them to survive, but I also wanted them to come home—not wander.

Something in the article on why dogs run away niggled at me. I knew neither Dickens nor Buttercup were bored or afraid, and I was pretty sure they weren't following any long-dormant mating or hunting instinct. But could Buttercup, not Dickens, be suffering from separation anxiety or feeling uncomfortable at my cottage because it was unfamiliar? Except Buttercup had also wandered away from the estate where she'd lived for several months. *Is she searching for Lucy?*

I didn't have an answer for that conundrum. The one thing I was convinced of was that Dickens's protective instinct had kicked in. Much as his breed protected goats and sheep, I was sure he had followed Buttercup to keep her safe.

Maybe I didn't have all the answers, but I did have an idea about spreading the word. I rang Wendy, hoping she was awake.

Not only was she up and about, she sounded chipper. "Mum went straight to bed, but I was wide awake. Would you believe I've been baking? What else was I going to do at dawn? I suspect I'll collapse after I get this last batch of biscuits out of the oven."

"That tells me I'll be stuffing flyers in letterboxes on my own. After reading this morning that dogs like Dickens and Buttercup can travel as far as 14 miles in a day, I've decided to visit villages beyond Bourton, like Little Rissington and Westcote."

"No way, Leta. It will take you all day on your own and will work much better if you drive and I hop out with the flyers. If we go now, we can be back in time for an afternoon nap before book club."

Our time together in the car gave me an opportunity to bring her up to speed on Ellie's plan and my morning surfing the internet.

"Mum was surprisingly lively last night. I expected her to fall asleep as soon as I parked the car, but she wanted to talk. She's quite proud of the work she and Ellie have done on the Canine Caper and took me through their investigation step by step."

Pulling up in front of another cottage, I looked at Wendy. "They were very methodical, though I'm not sure this stakeout business will produce results. What do you think?"

"I'm with you, but if it makes them happy, I'm willing to help. Not beyond tonight, though. If no one shows up tonight, I think we will have wasted enough time. Plus the snow may be here by Friday night, and we don't want to be out in that."

I dropped Wendy by her cottage and was back home by two. After wolfing down a plate of cheese and crackers, I revived the fire and collapsed on the couch with a throw tucked around my legs. It was time to let Dave know what I'd been up to.

His cheerful greeting was tinged with a note of concern. "Whenever you substitute texts for calls, it's a dead giveaway you're up to something. So, what is it this time?"

"I hope you have plenty of time because it's a long story." I was able to get through Belle and Ellie's Canine Caper presentation without much comment. It was when I got to the stakeout story that he reacted.

"A stakeout? You went on a stakeout, and it was their idea? I thought I could count on the two senior members of the team to be the voice of reason."

Wait until he hears about tonight's plan. "I think they've taken leave of their senses, but Wendy and I agreed we would play along for one more night."

He was less than happy when I explained the latest scenario, but his concern was somewhat mollified when he heard Peter would accompany Belle. And he was further distracted by the description of my wake-up call from Brian Burton.

"The man never changes, does he? Do you think he only attacks you like that, or is he an equal opportunity jerk?"

"You know, I've never considered that question, but I find it hard to believe that he's that much of a chameleon. What irks me is that I never seem to have a sharp witty 'put him in his place' retort ready when he attacks me. It's only later that I think of what I could have said."

Dave chuckled. "You know, the French have a phrase for that— l'esprit d'escalier."

"Show-off. What does it mean?"

"The literal translation is 'spirit of the staircase.' The comebacks you think of as you're leaving—walking down the stairs. I think of Parker's Spenser as the master of the comeback line and always wish I was that quick."

This is one reason we make such a good couple—our love of books. "Me too, or Sunny Randall, his female version of Spenser. She was great with witty one-liners too. Oh, and they both had dogs. What's not to like?"

My last comment brought me back to my biggest problem—Dickens. "Now, let me tell you what I found on the internet and how I've spent the last several hours."

We went back and forth about how far the dogs might have traveled and why. "Leta, I wonder if you're on to something about Buttercup. Could she be searching for Lucy? Maybe this is the first time Lucy's left for this length of time. I know some people believe dogs only live in the present, but if Buttercup was already missing Lucy's sister, Lucy leaving might have triggered something."

I bit my tongue. Dickens and Christie still talked about Henry, so I knew they remembered the past, but I couldn't tell Dave that. "Maybe I need to call Lucy and see what she thinks. She can't actively help from France, but she may be able to brainstorm with me."

After promising to call him Friday with a stakeout report, I stretched out on my side on the couch, and Christie tucked herself against my stomach beneath the throw. When people joked about what their superpower was, I always claimed mine was napping. I was exceptionally good at it.

CHAPTER ELEVEN

Christie studied me as I applied makeup. "What's that saying you humans have? You look like something the cat drug in."

"Is that your idea of a pep talk? All I want to do is crawl into bed, but I never miss book club, and then I have stakeout duty. I'm guaranteed to look even worse tomorrow."

When Wendy tooted the horn, I jogged down the stairs, grabbed my bag, and tossed it in her back seat. "How can you look so perky?"

Backing down the driveway, she blew out her breath. "It's an illusion. It's hard to believe I was ever able to party the night away and turn around and teach the next morning. What about you?"

"You have to ask? Ten is past my bedtime, much less two a.m., and I think my nap only made me feel worse. If someone is going to show up, let's hope it's by nine, and we can call it a night."

Beatrix was standing by the door to the Book Nook, looking anxious. "Thank goodness you two are here. It's not like you have to RSVP for book club, but lots of the regulars have called to say they're not coming. It seems everyone is preparing for the big storm."

There were only a handful of patrons milling around the shop, a few seated with glasses of wine and others perusing the tables of holiday books. As Trixie poured me a glass of wine, she inquired about Dickens and Buttercup and expressed her surprise about the call from Little Rissington.

Dressed in black, Ellie approached the counter with a stack of books. Tonight's sleuthing outfit took the form of slim black wool pants topped with a black cashmere turtleneck and short black boots. I pictured her tucking her silver hair into a black wool hat as she'd done the night before.

Rhiannon rushed in the door and took a seat with Gavin, Wendy, and me as Beatrix quieted the sparse crowd. As Ellie took her seat, our host introduced the December book club selection, *How to Find Love in a Bookshop*, and explained that she hadn't read the book until she and I stumbled across a copy of it in a cottage in Chipping Camden. She had quipped at the time that she had yet to find love in her bookshop.

She smiled at her audience. "I don't often read romance novels, but Leta assured me it was a charming book—not only a romance, but the perfect read for bibliophiles—and she was right. Of course, as a bookshop owner, I appreciated how the owner of Nightingale Books helped customers and friends choose books to suit their tastes and moods. As a reader, I reveled in the mention of books I too have enjoyed."

We joined her in a discussion of the characters and feel-good plot. It was a trip down memory lane for me when I spotted titles like *The World According to Garp* and *Rebecca* and authors like Ian Rankin, Ruth Rendell, and so many others I'd read through the years. Add the Cotswolds setting and the Christmas ending, and it was perfect.

As the group broke up, Trixie beckoned to me. "Leta, something stirred in the back of my mind when you said Dickens had been spotted in Little Rissington. Follow me."

In the small used-book section, she pulled out a slim leatherbound volume and handed it to me. My eyes widened at the title, *The Incredible Journey*. "Oh, I remember this book. I read it as a child." I flipped through it, recognizing the names of the two dogs and the cat—Bodger, Luath, and Tao—who traveled through the Canadian wilderness together. "I didn't realize the author was Scottish."

I hugged the book to my chest. Maybe Dave was on to something. Maybe Buttercup was searching for Lucy. The thought had barely taken shape in my brain when my phone lit up with a call. "Hello."

"Is this Leta Parker? I've got a sweet dog here with a red collar and tag that says he belongs to you. Name of Dickens."

Gasping, I gripped the phone. "You have Dickens. Oh my goodness, thank you. Is he okay?"

The man on the end of the line chuckled. "Other than being a bit dingy, I'd say he's fine. He's gobbled up two dishes of food, and now he's enjoying a belly rub."

I heard Dickens in the background barking and made out a few words—Buttercup, woods, food.

"Is there another dog with him? A short stocky golden retriever? They ran off together."

"Funny you should ask. This friendly boy came to the door, and I caught a glimpse of another dog near the tree line, but it wouldn't approach. And this one keeps going to the door as though he wants to leave. Is the other one yours too?"

I told him the story and asked if he would put the phone to Dickens's ear so I could talk to him. I cooed to Dickens and tried to ask questions in a way that wouldn't make my caller think I was a crazy lady. "Dickens, why did you leave? And where's Buttercup?"

It was difficult to understand his anxious answers. "Almost there. Tanya. Miss you."

What is he trying to tell me? My caller came back on the line and told me he lived in Idbury. "It's a bit late for me, and I need to turn in. I'll keep him overnight, and you can pick him up in the morning. The wife's allergic to dogs, so I'll make him comfortable in the shed with blankets and water."

"Um, I don't want to impose, but he's been missing since Monday. Is there any chance I can come to fetch him now? I can leave right away."

My caller was polite but firm as he reiterated his wish for a morning pickup. I wanted to run out the door and drive to his village, but I couldn't very well just show up, and I knew Dickens would be fine in the shed with his thick Great Pyrenees coat. What I wanted most was to have a conversation with Dickens to find out what was going on. As it was, I had only a few cryptic words to go on. I got the name of my caller—Charlie Pike—and his address, and we agreed I would call him in the morning when I was on my way.

Once again, I pictured a kindly white-haired gentleman dressed in a striped shirt and suspenders. It was such a vivid image, I was sure I must have seen it somewhere, and then

I remembered. Years ago, I'd fallen in love with a children's book while shopping with my sister Anna. The story about a neglected dog being adopted by an elderly widower touched my heart, and the illustrations were priceless. The title, *Lucky Boy*, said it all, and I couldn't resist buying a copy to take home. *I'll have to look for it on my bookshelf.*

I found Wendy in the stockroom, changing into a black outfit as she explained to Trixie what we were up to. Already dressed in black pants with a silky black top, all I had to do was exchange my red plaid cape for my quilted black parka and replace my red beret with my black cloche.

Beatrix walked in as I was assessing my look in her full-length mirror. "What on earth are you two up to? You look like something out of a comic strip."

Trixie grinned at her aunt. "Can you believe it? They're headed to a stakeout."

As she shared the sleuthing story with Beatrix, Wendy pulled her stocking cap over her platinum blonde hair. "Ready, Leta? Ellie's waiting outside with the Bentley."

Beatrix followed us to the front of the shop and stood in the doorway, muttering. The few words I could make out were, foolhardy, daft, and crazy, and in my heart, I agreed with her assessment of our latest scheme.

We drove past Peter's truck and waited for him and Belle to leave before Ellie backed the Bentley into the driveway and doused the lights. I'd given them the Dickens report on the way over. Like me, they wished Mr. Pike had agreed to let me pick up Dickens before the morning. The important thing was that my boy was safe, but I was concerned about Buttercup. Was she still looking for Lucy, or was she waiting for Dickens? Would she make an appearance in the morning when I arrived?

Knowing that Dickens was safe freed my brain to consider the information Belle and Ellie had collected. I doubted we'd surprise a clandestine visitor tonight, but even if we did, he or she would be only one piece of the puzzle—a less threatening piece.

Wendy must have been pondering the situation too. "Ellie, did you and Mum get your ransom report to Constable James yet?"

"We decided it needed a bit more polishing so that he's armed with everything he needs. We already knew DCI Burton wouldn't approve, but that became crystal clear when the man called Leta this morning. We're thinking that Jonas might want to conduct an off-the-books investigation on his own time."

Thank goodness. It had crossed my mind that our two senior citizens might be trying to hide their real plan from us—that they might be entertaining the idea of getting between a dog snatcher and his ransom money. "It makes me ill that no matter how much data you put at Jonas's fingertips, it's unlikely the perpetrators will be prosecuted. Based on what he told me, even if they are, the result would be a fine—not jail time."

Ellie didn't let my dismal outlook dampen her spirit. "You're right, Leta, but the capture and publicity might discourage others from giving it a try. I know that getting them to move on to greener pastures isn't a solution, but if we can scarper their local plans, we will have helped Astonbury and our neighboring villages in some small way."

That could very well put an end to the more sinister crime of stealing dogs and holding them for ransom, but how did it connect to the other notes, if at all? "And tonight? If anyone shows up and stuffs something in the letterbox, what will we learn?"

Wendy had a ready answer. "At a minimum, we'll discover the who, and with any luck, also the why."

Alarm bells went off in my head. "What do you mean, the why? I get following them and seeing where they live. And tomorrow, we can give Jonas the address so he can pay them a visit, but we won't know the why until . . . oh no! Don't tell me you think we're going to confront the person ourselves."

It was too dark to see their expressions, but I knew my friends were rolling their eyes. "Earth to Leta," Wendy said. "You didn't seriously think we'd stop at following the person home, did you?"

"Of course, I did. What are we going to do? Accost them in their driveway or at their front door? In the middle of the night?"

Ellie chuckled. "That's the plan, dear, unless you have a better one."

Wendy chimed in. "And that's why I brought Peter's cricket bat, just in case."

"This is my fault. I've been so focused on finding Dickens, I haven't paid enough attention to this stakeout thing."

As they both assured me they had things well in hand, an idea hit me. "Whoa, wait a minute.

Why do we have to follow anyone? Why don't we confront whoever it is as soon as they show up at Mrs. Miller's front door? Catch them in the act?"

Wendy snapped her fingers. "That could work unless they run. With your knees, you can't chase anyone, and I'm not very fast."

It was Ellie who put the pieces together. "Ladies, this person isn't going to walk here. They'll either arrive in a car or on a bicycle. As soon as they approach the front gate, you two can sneak over there while I move my car to block them in. Even if they run, it will be toward their vehicle, and I can blind them with my headlights. Yes, that's a much better plan than following them."

Laughing, Wendy agreed. "Trust you, Leta, to improve the plan."

We were debating whether to move to the garden and hide in the bushes when Ellie turned to me in the backseat. "Leta, do you still have the alarm Dave gave you?"

"Oh yes. That and the purple defensive spray. That thing is loud enough to wake the dead. Oh! I see where you're going. I should have one or both at the ready when we approach the front door. Wendy, we'll have to rely on you to wield your cricket bat if it becomes necessary."

It was now nine p.m. "Wendy, let's give the bushes a try. If it's too cold for us, we can always rejoin Ellie here."

Our plan paid off, but not before my feet turned to blocks of ice. It was nearly ten when a car turned onto the lane and parked. There was nothing suspicious about the driver turning off the engine and the lights, but I thought it telling that the car door was closed oh-so softly. When the tall figure approached Mrs. Miller's gate, I pulled my alarm and purple spray from my pockets.

He or she hesitated before they reached the pool of light at the front door, perhaps deciding whether to risk being exposed. When a hand reached for the letterbox, Wendy and I emerged from the bushes on either side of the path.

Holding the cricket bat in both hands, Wendy said, "Stop right there. Don't move."

At the sound of her voice, the figure swung around. Something about it was familiar, but I couldn't quite make out the face. When a white envelope fell to the ground, I took a chance and reached in to snatch it, and so did the hooded figure.

Our heads bumped as we both grabbed for the envelope, and I heard a male voice. "No!"

With his hood in reach, I was able to push it off his head. "Ric?"

Dropping the envelope, he stumbled backward and put a hand on the door. "Leta? What are you doing here?"

"The question is, what are *you* doing here?"

"I, um, I came to talk to Mrs. Miller." He hesitated and looked at Wendy. "About her missing dog."

We must have been quite a tableau—me brandishing defensive spray, Wendy with her cricket bat, and Ric standing frozen in front of us. When he hesitantly put one foot in front of the other, a voice rang out. "Hands in the air." An expression of horror appeared on Ric's face as he raised his arms high. "Now, turn around and place your hands on the door."

Is that who I hope it is? I understood the look of horror on Ric's face when I glanced behind me and saw Ellie brandishing a shotgun. "Oh my gosh, Ellie, where did you get that?"

"It's from Nigel's collection. Wendy, get Mrs. Miller's spare key from my pocket, please, and open the door."

As Ellie held the muzzle against Ric's back, Wendy unlocked the door and turned the latch. Ric stumbled inside, and we followed.

This was a side of Ellie I'd never seen. She steered Ric to the couch and barked, "Sit." She told me to take the easy chair and instructed Wendy to make tea. Only after tea was served did she sit on a wooden chair by the desk and rest the shotgun across her lap. "I heard Leta call you Ric. Would you care to explain yourself?"

White as a sheet, Ric struggled to form words. I realized that I had picked up the envelope when he pointed to my lap. "Leta, open it. It will help explain."

I opened it and read the words aloud. *Please be more careful with your dog.* "Ric, what does this mean?"

He gulped. "It's, it's harmless."

Wendy erupted. "Harmless? You leave alarming notes for dog owners, and you call that harmless?"

Motioning Wendy to hush, I nodded at Ric. "Explain that, please. Why are you, of all people, stealing dogs?"

"I'm not stealing them—well not exactly. I started out returning lost dogs to their owners. I run the country lanes and cycle the area too. Twice, I came upon dogs wandering along the verge, in danger of being hit by a car. Both times, I checked their tags and took them home, and both times their owners were overjoyed and insisted on paying me for my trouble. And I never kept a penny for myself; I gave it all to Pepper's."

"What changed?"

He ran his hands through his hair. "The third time, I was really irked that the poor dog didn't have a tag. We see so many lost dogs at the shelter, and most of them are never claimed. I took him to Pepper's and checked for a chip, and when I located the owner's information, I discovered that the phone had been disconnected. I mean, how irresponsible! But when I checked the *Astonbury Aha,* there he was—Georgie, last seen at 112 Farmingdale Lane."

Tilting my head, I studied him. Wendy would say I was working the pregnant pause.

It had the desired effect. In a moment, Ric ducked his head and continued. "It was past eleven and too late to call that night, so I bathed him at the shelter and took him home with me. We watched the telly together, and when I woke the next day, I had an idea. It was kind of a combination of the mystery I watched the night before and the book, *Pepper's Pies.*"

Wendy spoke up. "*Pepper's Pies.* Why does that sound familiar?"

Ric grew animated as he explained the storyline and how the book funded the shelter. "It's because of that children's book that we have a shelter at all, but we're running out of money."

Smiling, Wendy wondered aloud whether Belle still had the book at Sunshine Cottage with her other childhood books. She squinted at Ric. "But you didn't take this dog. You found it. What am I missing?"

"The first two owners were so eager to pay me, I wondered how much more Georgie's owner would give me if he had a bit of an incentive. Instead of a piece of pie, maybe I'd get more money. I got the idea for the note from the show on the telly, and I spelled out, 'Don't you love your dog,' in letters from some old magazines. Stuffed the note in the letterbox the next night and called the owner in the morning to say I had Georgie. It worked like a charm. I couldn't believe it when he gave me £60."

When Ellie shifted her shotgun and leaned toward him, he blanched. "Ric, are you trying to tell us this is all an altruistic scheme to help the shelter?"

"Yes ma'am. I haven't found any dogs on the road in a few weeks, but when a dog is brought into the shelter on my shift, I check the *Astonbury Aha* for a lost dog alert. It's easy as pie—I can't believe I said that. I mean it's simple to do. If I find a match, I take the dog home with me, put together a note, and stuff it in the letterbox, that very night if I can. I give it twelve or twenty-four hours and then make the call. It's bloody brilliant. One owner gave me £100."

He ducked his head. "And some of these owners are repeat offenders. If my notes make them take better care of their pets, then what's the harm?"

All I could do was shake my head. It *was* a simple scheme, and his heart was in the right place. Still, I tried to put myself in Mrs. Miller's place. With Dickens missing, how would I feel if I got a note straight out of a mystery novel—one that implied that I didn't take good care of my dog? Ric had lost sight of the fact that not all lost pets had irresponsible owners. Sometimes, stuff just happened.

Wendy didn't seem convinced. "How do we know you're telling the truth? That you didn't take a page from *Pepper's Pies* and take these dogs yourself? Even if it was to get money for the shelter, that would be unforgivable."

Ric's mouth dropped open. "I—I would never do anything like that. Yes, I hoped to get a bit of extra dosh for the shelter, but in the end, all the dogs were reunited with their owners. As for the few who didn't give me any kind of reward? They got their lost dogs back and maybe learned a lesson too."

Is he pulling the wool over our eyes? "What about Tank? Did you really find him in the churchyard? That's what you told his owner."

"Yes, I did. I heard him whimpering as I cycled past, and I took him to the shelter to bathe him and figure out who his owner was."

"But Ric, I understand it was a young girl who returned him. Not you."

He put his hands on his thighs. "I can explain that. It was Polly. I planned to take him, but we were swamped at the shelter that night, and it was Polly's night off. I called and asked her if she could take him home. She had no idea about the note or anything else." He paused. "She was so pleased that she got £20. She told me all about it the next day and stuffed it in the Pepper's jar at Posh Pets. Not everyone has lots of money to give, but every little bit helps."

Looking at Ellie and Wendy, I suggested the three of us convene in the kitchen. "Ric, I suggest you stay put unless you want us to call the police right away."

Wendy propped her hip against the counter. "I'm inclined to believe him. What do you ladies think?"

I cleared my throat. "Well, it wouldn't be the first time I misjudged someone, but I agree with you.

He couldn't make up a story like that on the spot, and I doubt he had it prepared."

We pulled his words apart looking for inconsistencies but found only one. It was the bit about where he found Bingo—on the other side of town. Bob Weir was puzzled about that, and so were we. Returning to the sitting room, I questioned him about seeing the small dog on the road to Bourton.

"Oh! I was on my way to Bourton to pick up supplies for the shelter when I spotted him, and good thing I did. He'd been missing for days."

With that settled, the three members of the Little Old Ladies' Detective Agency agreed we were willing to give him the benefit of the doubt. We might not approve of his methods, but he hadn't broken any laws. He hadn't snatched any dogs, and he hadn't sent ransom notes. According to Ric, all the animals had been returned to their owners. The truth is that a few of them might have stayed at the shelter longer if not for his taking the extra step to check the *Astonbury Aha*. And goodness knows what would have happened to Bingo.

The next question was what to do with him. Scrunching her mouth to the side, Wendy made a pronouncement. "I say we get him to solemnly swear to stop these shenanigans, and we leave it at that. I see no reason to turn him into the police. I mean, what purpose would that serve?"

"None at all," I said. "I doubt it's a crime to put anonymous notes in letterboxes. It's no different than slipping a flyer in one."

Ellie agreed. "Okay. That's settled. And I can see a happy ending to this part of the Canine Caper. I plan to find out how much money Pepper's needs to stay afloat and fund it immediately. After that, I'll work with the shelter to determine a long-term solution to the problem."

Wendy grinned at me. "I see a fundraiser in our future, and maybe a few feel-good stories on the

Astonbury Aha. People love your columns, and
they love animals, so what could be better than a
series on pets?"

"Oooh. That's right up my alley. And to give it
a different twist, it could be a series written by
Dickens and Christie. What fun!"

Glancing at Ellie, Wendy chuckled. "Honest
to goodness, I think she understands those two
anyway. I can't wait to see what words she puts in
their mouths."

Ellie laughed. "Now, Wendy, you know I
understand Blanche and Watson. Their language
is limited to a few key demands—feed me, rub
my belly, let me out, let me in. What's not to
understand?"

A male voice interrupted our chatter. "Um, does
the laughter mean you've forgiven me?"

Squaring her shoulders and pasting a solemn
expression on her face, Ellie marched into the
sitting room with us behind her. I had to stifle

a laugh when she launched into her dowager
countess act.

"Young man, this is no laughing matter. We are
not going to turn you in, but we have several
requirements you must meet. Should you fail to
uphold your end of the bargain, rest assured, we
will see to it that the full power of the law comes
to bear."

If the look of relief on his face was any indication,
I suspected Ric had no idea there was very little
the police could do to him. He eagerly committed
to doing everything Ellie laid out. Cease the
anonymous notes, call Mrs. Miller first thing in
the morning and return Panda, accompany Ellie
to meet with the manager of the shelter about
Pepper's finances, and pretty much be at her beck
and call for the foreseeable future. I expected him
to prostrate himself at Lady Stow's feet any minute.
It was all I could do to keep a straight face.

The evening had been a success in so many ways. We ladies had solved the mystery of at least one part of the Canine Caper. Pepper's Animal Shelter would receive an infusion of cash to see them through the next few months, plus the promise of future help. And more importantly to me, I knew where Dickens was.

CHAPTER TWELVE

WITHOUT DICKENS TO GREET me at the door, my arrival at my cottage was a quiet one. It would take Christie a moment to wake up, but I knew she would appear soon. I hung my parka in the boot room, shook the wrinkles out of my cape, and brewed a cup of chamomile tea. No matter that it was late, I was too keyed up to go to bed.

A sleepy meow echoed down the stairs. "Where have you been? You're late."

As she twined between my legs, I scratched her head. "Who are you? My mom?"

I spooned a dab of wet food into her dish and sat at the kitchen table. "We'll have Dickens home tomorrow, little girl."

That news got her attention, and she leaped onto my lap. Instead of curling up, she stood on my legs and reached her paw to my chin. "Where is he? I miss him."

She meowed questions and comments as I gave her the short version. "You're going to give him a talking-to, aren't you, Leta? He's been a bad dog."

"Yes, Christie. By the way, did Watson come by tonight?"

"No, but he's bound to show up sooner or later. Unless he's hanging out in Bourton at restaurants."

"What makes you say that?"

"I've been thinking about what Paddington's friend Punky said and wondering whether the cat she saw could have been Watson."

That idea hadn't crossed my mind. When his owner in Chipping Camden died, Libby and Gavin took him in, but, of his own accord, Watson decided to take up residence with Ellie at the manor house. I doubted any of us knew how far he wandered on his nightly adventures.

"Does he go that far?"

"Don't know. He visits the inn and the pub and the donkey barn, but there's no telling where else he goes." She licked her paw and looked up at me. "It's not like I miss him, you know."

"Methinks the lady doth protest too much."

"Whatever that means. Can I go with you to get Dickens?"

"We'll see. Now it's time for me to call Dave." I carried my cape and my bookshop purchase to the bedroom and changed into my flannel nightgown. As I dialed Dave, I stared at the cloudy sky and wondered when the snow would come in. The Cotswolds weather forecasters seemed much like those in Atlanta—it would be a horrendous storm or nothing at all, and when it would hit was up for debate.

He answered the phone on the first ring. "Leta, are you okay? I thought you'd never call."

I'd forgotten that the last thing I'd told him was that I was going on a stakeout. "Oh, Dave, I'm sorry. Everything is fine. And I have good news about Dickens."

As I wound down, he said exactly what I'd been thinking all night. "I can't believe you didn't take off to get him, but I understand. If Mr. Pike asked you to wait, there wasn't much you could do. I imagine there's a stern talking-to and bath in Dickens's future. Am I right?"

How funny that he and Christie thought the same thing. "Yes, and I still need to locate Buttercup. It had to be her that Mr. Pike saw lurking near the tree line. I can only hope she'll still be there in the morning. Now, on a different note, let me tell you about the successful stakeout."

"Successful stakeout? I guess since you're talking calmly and you're not calling from an emergency room, that means it was also safe? Or is the phrase 'safe stakeout' an oxymoron?"

"You word nerd. That's more than I can deal with this late at night." I explained it all, and I even got a chuckle when I told him about Ellie's shotgun.

"I guess if she was carrying it, she must know how to use it. Did you ask if it was loaded?"

"You know, that question never occurred to me. I'll have to ask her tomorrow. Funny, I have an image of her shooting grouse like they did on *Downton Abbey*, except the women weren't allowed to shoot."

"It sounds like you were the voice of reason. Can you imagine what might have happened if Ellie and Wendy had been on their own? They'd have gone haring after this Ric fellow without a second thought and accosted him at his home. With Ellie carrying a shotgun, there's no telling what his reaction would have been."

"Admit it, I'm almost always the voice of reason. It's Wendy who's the risk-taker. As for Ellie, I'm not sure what got into her about this stakeout thing."

We wrapped up with a joking debate about who was more reasonable, and I promised to call him as soon as I was on the way home with Dickens.

With Christie curled by my side, I turned off the light. I was exhausted, but I tossed and turned. Thoughts of what I would tell Lucy if I couldn't find Buttercup mingled with worries about dognappers. Finally, I switched on the light and pulled out the book Trixie had found.

As I flipped through it, I marveled at the black and white sketches that brought the story to life. I'd forgotten that the cat Tao played such an important role in *The Incredible Journey*. The three companions looked out for each other, but the Siamese cat was especially protective of Bodger, the older dog.

Two dogs and a cat. Could Watson be with Dickens and Buttercup? Is that even remotely possible? I dozed off with the book open on my chest and dreamed of Watson guiding Buttercup along a stream.

Once again, I was awakened by an early-morning call. My book fell to the floor and Christie meowed a complaint as I reached for the phone. "Hello."

"This is Charlie Pike. Sorry to wake you."

I didn't exactly bolt upright, but I tried. "What? Is something wrong?"

"Yes. I can't explain how it happened, but it seems your dog is an escape artist." As he told his story, my emotions alternated between dismay and astonishment.

"When I put your boy in the shed with a bowl of water last night, I saw the other dog again, and the two barked at each other, so I returned with a second bowl of water and one of food. If that one was anywhere near as hungry as Dickens, I knew it needed food.

"This morning, I took a big bowl of kibble with me to the shed, thinking I'd feed Dickens and refill the other bowl too. I was half hoping I could coax the other one into the shed to wait for you. Instead, I found the shed door hanging open. When I swung my flashlight toward my neighbor's yard, I glimpsed three shadows disappearing in the distance."

"Three shadows?"

"Yes. The third one was much smaller, and for some reason, I wondered if it might be a cat. Maybe the way it moved."

"Mr. Pike, did they seem to be moving farther away from Astonbury?"

"I'm sorry to say they did. None of the villages around Idbury are very large, but as a marker for you, I'd say they seem to be heading in the direction of Bledington—the opposite direction from you. Not that it makes a difference, but Bledington's population is about twice that of Idbury."

None of those names were familiar to me, as I didn't often get beyond Stow or Chipping Camden in that direction, but something was stirring in the back of my mind.

"Is there a village named Kingwood or Kingley or something like that?"

"There's Kingham, about 6 kilometers from here. What about it?"

"That's it. It's where Buttercup, the other dog, lived before moving to Astonbury. Maybe I'm clutching at straws, but I wonder if she's trying to get to her old home."

Mr. Pike cleared his throat. "I think we underestimate animals, and we don't give them enough credit for their instincts. Kingham may well be the destination. The missus and I have friends there. I'll give them a call and ask them to be on the lookout. Sorry I didn't have better news this morning." He chuckled. "When you find the rascals, would you please ask them how they unlatched the shed door?"

I assured him I would, right after I asked why they left in the first place. *Now, what do I do?*

When I googled kilometers to miles, I found that Kingham was around 3.5 miles from Idbury. Based on what I'd read about how far dogs could travel in a day, that was an easy distance for the travelers. Except, surely, they were getting worn out. It was too early to wake Lucy in France, but finding out the address of the Kingham cottage was a logical next step.

I didn't have a fully formulated plan, but I wanted to be prepared for whatever the day might hold. With that in mind, I poured Christie's puddle of milk, grabbed a mug of coffee, and headed upstairs to shower. Today, I had no time for checking emails and playing Words with Friends.

Christie was eager to pick up Dickens and was none too pleased when I told her about his Houdini act. "Again, he ran away *again*? What's wrong with him?" She bathed herself and grumbled about her canine brother as I showered and dressed.

I called Lucy at seven. "I wish I could say I had the dogs back, but I may be close."

When I mentioned Idbury and what had transpired there, she recalled what a lovely hamlet it was. "But it's 16 kilometers away. Nearly to Kingham."

"Exactly. And I have a wild thought. Could Buttercup be working her way to Kingham, where you lived before?"

"Hmm. It's possible. She lived in that cottage with Tanya for nearly ten years. Tanya died. We moved to Astonbury, and I left for France. Maybe she thinks I'm not coming back either." She paused. "I think it makes sense, Leta. Dogs are remarkable creatures."

"Phew. I'm glad you don't think I'm crazy. What's the situation with the cottage? Do you know whether anyone lives there now? Regardless, I'm going to drive to the village to see what I can find out."

Lucy gave me the address of her sister's cottage and the name and number of the nearest neighbor. "The cottage is on the market, but it hasn't sold yet. It held so many sad memories for me that I couldn't stay. I wanted to remember Tanya in her better days."

"That's understandable. I was the same way when my husband died. I downsized to a condo, and then I left altogether and moved here. It was the best decision I ever made." I promised to keep her posted, and then I called Sarah.

Explaining the Idbury to Kingham scenario took some time, and then I got to the point. "Sarah, I want to drive to Kingham in search of the dogs, but I don't think I should take my London taxi. The forecasters are now saying the snow will hit tonight, but if they're a few hours off, I would hate to get stuck out on the road. What are the chances you and I could go in your Land Rover?"

Sarah wanted to help, but she was working with Susan to move the sheep in preparation for the snow. "It's not that they can't weather the storm, but it's easier for us to get to them when they're in the barn. I don't have a problem with you taking the Land Rover on your own, though. Do you think Gavin or Peter would go with you?"

Peter was torn. "Crikey, Leta, it's a madhouse here at the garage. Panic mode has set in among the visitors from the city, and I'm trying to see to my regulars too. But you have no business being out on the road by yourself. I know you're worried

about Dickens, but this is his kind of weather."
The only way I could get him off the phone was to
promise I'd find someone else to go with me. I let
his admonishment to be sure it was a man pass. I
agreed with him on that score. If we got stuck in the
snow, a man with a shovel would come in handy.

I was about to call Gavin when I had a
brainstorm. When I called Ellie with the idea, she
was all for it. "That young man owes us, and he'll
bend over backward to help in any way he can.
Besides, he likes dogs. I'll ring Posh Pets and get
right back to you."

The sky was that eerie steel grey that indicated
snow was coming, and no one had driven down
Schoolhouse Lane in the last hour. Villagers were
taking the warnings seriously.

The number for Posh Pets appeared on my cell
phone. "Leta, it's Ric. Looks like I'm your driver
for the day. Lady Stow sorted it with Mindy, and
I'm on my way to you. People have been ringing

nonstop this morning to cancel their grooming appointments, so Mindy's closing early, and I'm not due at the shelter until the late shift—if I'm even able to get there."

It was time to break out my fur-lined snow boots and add an extra blanket to Christie's backpack. Ric's mouth dropped open when I exited the cottage with Christie, but he took it in stride. "A new client, is she?"

I texted Ellie that we were on the way and was surprised when she called me. "I'll meet you at the carriage house with tea, sandwiches, and jugs of water for the dogs. I'm going with you." She hung up before I could respond.

A fashionable petite snow bunny emerged from the carriage house as we pulled up. Ellie's silver hair peeked from the fur-trimmed hood of a hiplength quilted jacket. The sleeves were also trimmed in fur, as were her tall black lace-up boots.

Hopping from Ric's car, I called, "I am clearly underdressed for this event."

She laughed. "These old things? It seemed like the perfect opportunity to drag out the clothes I wore when Nigel and I skied in Switzerland. I'm just happy they still fit."

"Ellie, I know you're dressed appropriately for the weather, but are you sure you want to do this? It's one thing for me to get stuck somewhere, but I'm pretty sure Matthew and Sarah would never forgive me if you did too."

"Rubbish. I'll be perfectly fine." She looked at Ric. "You, young man, don't have nearly enough layers on. Wait one minute."

She pulled out her cell phone and spoke to Caroline about a jacket for Ric. In no time, I saw Caroline at the kitchen entrance holding another black jacket and what looked like a fur Cossack hat. Ellie sent Ric to fetch the garments and turned to me. "He's tall like Nigel was, so I think the jacket will do, and it pays to have a decent hat in this weather."

Ric held the hat at arm's length. "You don't expect me to wear this, do you?"

Ellie's response was suitably stern. "As needed, yes."

Passing Peter's garage reminded me I needed to let him know I'd found a driver. I texted him the plan and said I'd be in touch. At the same time, Ellie texted Wendy to let her know we were on the road. We'd covered all our bases.

Ric was a careful driver and a cheerful one. He entertained us with stories of some of the more outrageously pampered pets and their very picky parents—the kind that Mindy often threatened to ban from Posh Pets. "It's most often the weekenders, but every so often, it's a local. Mindy's good at dealing with them, better than I'll ever be."

As light snow began to fall, I thought of the storms I'd experienced in Atlanta. The city never failed to be unprepared. One year, I had to leave my car parked at my downtown office and trudge through the snow to my home in Virginia-Highland. Thankfully, I had worn my heavy winter coat and winter boots that day, so the three-mile trek was more of an adventure than an ordeal. I worked with people who never wore winter coats and wound up spending the night freezing in their cars on the side of the road.

Ellie insisted on sitting in the back seat with Christie so I would have the best view of the road. She'd brought along her Canine Caper report and was scribbling notes as we rode.

I turned to her. "How's it going, Ellie? Is it perfect yet?"

"Not quite. It feels like so little to go on. Yes, we have the ransom drop location and where the dogs are left, but I wish we had something more about the dog snatchers. A description of a person or a vehicle."

Ric looked in the rearview mirror. "Lady Stow, I've been thinking, and I may have something for you. You know how I told you I picked Bingo up on this road? I didn't want to get into it, but I found him because I saw someone toss him from a van—at least, that's what I think I saw."

My mouth dropped open. "You what?"

"I know. It's unbelievable, isn't it? The van slowed and pulled off the road in front of me. When I passed it, I thought I saw a blur of white on the verge before they picked up speed and came around me. Something made me turn around, and that's when I spotted Bingo."

Ellie sat forward. "I don't suppose you saw the license plate, did you?"

"Only the first letter—an M—which made me think maybe it was a Manchester plate. I was more focused on it being an ancient Volkswagen—one of those two-colored ones. Some call them minibuses instead of vans. You don't see many of those."

A grin broke out on Ellie's face. "Ric, what two colors?"

"Maybe aqua and white. It was beat-up and dirty."

"Perfect! I'll add that and type up the report when we get back. Maybe it's not connected to the ransom notes, but what if it is? If Jonas can ID the owner and question him, we'll at least know who snatched Bingo—or who bought him."

I was following her line of thought and recalled Bob saying that Bingo was elderly. Whoever took him could have realized that and tossed him away like trash, or they could have sold him to someone equally cruel. It was enough to make a person lose all faith in humanity.

As we approached the outskirts of Bourton, the wind picked up, and the snow grew heavier. Bourton-on-the-Water was beautiful year-round, but at Christmas, it outdid itself. The lighted Christmas tree in the middle of the River

Windrush was its star attraction, at least to me. Now, with the snow falling, it was picture perfect.

We took the road to Little Rissington, where Dickens had been spotted earlier in the week. It was a picturesque drive, and Ric took it slowly. I wanted to see where Dickens had spent the night to see if it offered any additional clues. The snow was a bit heavier now and beginning to stick to the road as well as the fields. It wasn't long before we found Charlie Pike's cottage.

It was a tidy homestead with a stone fence bordering the front garden and a cheerful holiday wreath on the front door. Behind the cottage, I caught a glimpse of the shed, and further back, the trees bordered by a post and rail fence. A man I assumed to be Charlie was trundling wood from the shed to the cottage as we pulled up. He must have heard us because he came around to the front and waved.

As I emerged from the Land Rover, he hollered a cheerful greeting. "You must be Leta. Have you come to see the scene of the crime?"

"That, and to thank you for calling me. Have you figured out how Dickens escaped?"

With introductions made, he escorted us to the shed. "It's a simple latch, but it opens from the outside, so I'm stumped. Maybe I didn't shut it well enough, but I think it would have swung open behind me if that were the case."

The shed door was bordered by two large windows with flower boxes beneath them. "What a lovely setting. And you say the animals were traveling in the direction of Bledington?"

He pointed to his right. "Yes, and if Kingham's their destination, they may be there by now. I hope you find them before the snow gets any heavier."

I thanked him profusely, and we all piled back into Ellie's Land Rover. The Google map told me it was an eight-minute drive to Kingham—but not today. The halfway mark was the hamlet of Foscot, and it took us twenty minutes to get there.

I'd seen pictures of what we were experiencing. It didn't take much snow accumulation for the narrow Cotswolds lanes flanked by high stone walls to become nearly impassable. Fingers crossed it wouldn't be that bad today.

When Christie meowed my name, I glanced in the backseat. "What is it, little girl?"

"Let me out. I want to help."

"Ellie, would you mind taking Christie out of the backpack. She seems to be getting anxious."

"Pfft. I'm not anxious. I want to help."

Unlatching the clasp, Ellie made soothing sounds and transferred Christie to her lap. "There, there, it will be okay. Do you miss Dickens?"

"I think she does, Ellie. She's an independent little thing, but she and Dickens have been together since she was a kitten."

Christie stood on her hind legs and pressed her pink nose to the side window. "It's cold! We need to find them."

She chose that moment to leap from Ellie's lap to the top of my seat and was in my lap in a flash. I whispered in her ear, "We'll be there soon."

Another thirty minutes, and we arrived in Kingham. We drove along Church Street with its mix of cottages and houses, all in the honey-gold stone so prevalent in the Cotswolds. "Ellie, how have I missed this village? I've seen two pubs and quite a few shops. When this is all over, we need to plan a day trip."

We followed the directions on my phone to a small thatched cottage on the outskirts of the village. Beyond it, I glimpsed rolling hills blanketed in snow. Pulling into the gravel driveway, Ric turned off the motor.

This was it. If they weren't here, I didn't know what our next step would be. Knock on the doors of the neighboring cottages, the ones with smoke curling from their chimneys? Sit and wait?

I put my lips to Christie's ear and whispered, "You wait here until I check things out. You can watch from the dashboard."

Taking a deep breath, I stepped gingerly into the snow. I was shutting the door when I was distracted by a streak of color flying my way. With a loud meow, the streak leaped onto my chest and clung to my quilted jacket.

"Watson? Is that you?" I dusted the snow off the tabby as he tried to tuck his head into my hood."

When Ellie emerged from the car, he craned his neck in her direction. "Did you bring food? We're hungry."

Pulling her wayward cat into her arms, Ellie stroked his head. "Watson, what on earth are you doing here?"

He nuzzled the fur around Ellie's hood. "I couldn't let Buttercup go off on her own. She doesn't see well."

That confirmed my suspicion that it was Buttercup who instigated the big adventure. "Watson, please tell me Dickens is with you too."

Ellie gave me a strange look, which reminded me she had no clue that Watson's meows meant something to me—that I now knew for sure the three animals had traveled as a unit. "Ellie, don't you see, Watson must have followed Buttercup, and I can only hope the two dogs are still together."

The next sound to disturb the quiet landscape was Dickens's joyous bark. "Leta, Leta, here I am." Barreling into my legs, the bundle of dingy white fur knocked me into the snow and climbed onto my chest. "You're here. You're here. I knew you'd come."

"Oh my gosh, Dickens, you don't know how glad I am to see you. Where's Buttercup? She's with you, right?"

He licked my face and barked. "Come with me. She needs help." He didn't wait for a response before leaping from my chest and darting behind the cottage with Ric in close pursuit.

By now, only Christie remained in the Land Rover, and her howls told me that she was *not* happy. Grabbing her from the front seat, I fell into line behind Ric, and Ellie brought up the rear with a squirming Watson in her arms.

Pawprints and barking led us to an architectural delight in the back garden. There, tucked against the low stone wall, stood a pale blue shed with white-trimmed windows and a small veranda. Sheer white curtains with embroidered bluebells hung in the windows. "Ellie, look at that. It looks like a playhouse made for adults."

Ric was kneeling by a doghouse on the veranda painted the same pale blue, a miniature version of the shed. "Leta, Lady Stow, you're not going to believe this."

When I stepped onto the veranda, I saw a wooden sign hanging over the doghouse doorway and glimpsed two furballs inside. Carved on the sign was the name Buttercup.

"Oh my goodness, Ric, I can't see. Is Buttercup okay? Is she moving?"

As Ric examined Buttercup the best he could, Dickens stuck his head out and answered my question. "It's her paw. She hurt her paw this morning."

Dickens, ever the protector, looked at me as he nudged Buttercup's left hind paw. "Can we fix it, Leta? Can we make it better?"

"Leta," said Ric, "I'm no vet, but I think she's okay except for her paw. I don't see a wound, but she whimpers when I touch it."

Buttercup whined. "I'm home, but where's Tanya? Where's Lucy?"

Ellie came up behind me. "You were right, Leta. Buttercup set out to find her home. Poor thing. She must be heartbroken."

Sitting back on his haunches, Ric murmured, "It's like that movie I saw as a lad. What was it? *Homeward Bound,* where the three animals set out to find their owners?"

I looked at Ellie. "I never saw the movie. What I remember is the book it was based on. It was Trixie showing me an ancient copy of *The Incredible Journey* last night that made me wonder if that's what was going on with Buttercup. In the book, the animals find their family. Poor Buttercup. She doesn't understand that Lucy is her only family now."

For a moment, the three of us were lost in our separate thoughts, and it took Christie jumping from my arms to stir me to action.

"Goodness, it's time we headed home. Dickens, let Ric get to Buttercup, and we'll be on our way. Ric, can you carry her to the car?"

Dickens led the way to the Land Rover, and Ellie opened the boot and made a bed of the blankets we'd brought. Watson leaped in as Ric laid Buttercup down and tucked the covers around her.

As I secured Christie in her backpack, she meowed, "Dickens, you sit with me. I missed you."

With Ellie and Watson in the front seat, Dickens and I joined Christie in the back. Buttercup lay quietly on her nest of blankets. She had to be worn out, and I hoped there was nothing wrong with her beyond her paw and fatigue.

Ric and Ellie conferred in the front seat as I nuzzled Dickens and used a towel to dry his wet fur. I only half listened as Ric called the vet in Stow and established that she was spending the night rather than fighting the storm to get to her flat.

My companions decided we would take a different route home, one that would take us through Stow. With that settled, Ric focused on driving.

The smell of wet dog permeated the car, but none of us seemed to mind. Even Christie had no complaints.

Watson left Ellie's lap to check out Christie in her backpack "Is there room in there for me?" He didn't wait for an answer before squirming in beside her.

Ellie and I laughed at the loud purring that ensued as Christie washed Watson's face. All was well in the cat kingdom.

"Leta, can you hand me my Canine Caper report, please? Since we'll be in Stow, let's see whether Constable James is on duty. If he is, I think we should drop this by the station, even though it's not nice and neat. What do you think?"

Ric glanced at me in the rearview mirror. "Um, ladies, the roads are getting more treacherous by the minute. We have to get Buttercup to the vet, but after that, I think we need to head to Astonbury as quickly as we can."

As if to give credence to his suggestion, the Land Rover hit a patch of ice, and Ric only narrowly avoided sliding into a snow-covered fence. Ellie and I agreed he had a point, so I suggested she call the police station in Stow to see if she could talk Jonas through her findings instead.

She was in luck. Jonas had been on the overnight shift Thursday but had offered to stay on after hearing the weather report. Things were relatively quiet, but he knew that was bound to change. "DI Taylor's here too. She's due to go off duty in an hour, but since she doesn't have four-wheel drive, I think she's staying."

Ellie let him know he was on speakerphone before she took him through her findings. He was appropriately impressed with the work she and Belle had done. "The cricket pavilion? Are you kidding?" His next words were muffled as though he'd put his hand over the phone, and then he asked Ellie to hold on.

When he came back on the line, he explained he had stepped into the stairwell. "I didn't want to chance DI Taylor overhearing me, but you know it would be child's play to lay a trap for them—if only we had the manpower, but we don't. And, besides, you know what DCI Burton would think of that idea."

When Ellie got to the part about the Volkswagen van, he let out a whoop. "Blimey, this is perfect timing. I'm not on the clock right now, so I can start checking the description and maybe call a mate in Manchester to see if they have anything on it. There's a fair number of minibuses out there, but aqua and white ones are rare."

"Jonas, this is Leta. If you're able to identify them or even catch them in the act, what can you do? You made it pretty clear it's a minor offense."

"That depends. Chances are they're involved in more than a spot of dognapping, and if that's the case, something else may come of this. I'll see what I can find on my own, and if there's more, then DCI Burton can't complain."

I could only shake my head. I knew better. The man had an uncanny knack for finding fault in everything and everyone, but he wasn't my problem today. I had more pressing matters to attend to—like getting Buttercup medical attention.

CHAPTER THIRTEEN

WHAT SHOULD HAVE BEEN no more than a fifteen-minute journey took nearly an hour, but we finally made it to the vet. Ric carried Buttercup into the back as Ellie and I sat in the waiting room. Fortunately, we were the only customers.

Ric appeared out front and said Dr. Osborne wanted to see me, so we traded places. It turned out she had seen Buttercup before and was the vet who treated her when she had her bout with vestibular disease. She wanted to hear the details of when the dogs disappeared and how I surmised where to find them.

After listening attentively, she smiled. "I am so glad you figured it out. People don't want to believe it, but older dogs can develop doggie dementia, as we call it, especially after coming through something like old dog disease. Not long after that, I had to put her under to remove a growth on her hip. It's not unlike an elderly human patient who has surgery. It can be a difficult recovery when you're older, and humans and canines alike can be left disoriented."

When I shared my story about Banjo and his permanent head tilt, she chuckled. "Did he wobble too?"

"Oh yes, and over his last six months, he would wake up in the middle of the night and bark for no reason. He was never really the same. Of course, when he barked, I always worried he needed to go out. Picture me going downstairs at two or three a.m. to find him lying by the front door barking and wanting nothing more than a belly rub."

"And you gave him one and told him you loved him, right? It's what we do. Well, the good news about Buttercup is she's only sprained her paw. It's not broken. I'm going to wrap it, and you can take her home. I suggest Lucy keep her on a leash for the next month and then see how she does. That's so she doesn't run off again. It's not about her paw."

"Thank goodness. Do you think she'll learn to stay close after being kept more confined?"

"I can't promise anything, but she'll likely adjust. I think it may have been too much change for her all at once, and Lucy leaving for more than a day may have tipped the scales. Time will tell."

In the waiting room, I gave Ellie and Ric the report. "You know, Ellie, I bet Lucy didn't bring Buttercup's doghouse with her because it was just too big to move easily. After the storm passes, maybe Peter and I can take his truck to get it."

I stifled a laugh when Ellie looked meaningfully at Ric. He got the message. "I can help. It's pretty large and kind of unwieldy, and will take two men to shift it. No offense meant, Leta."

"None taken, Ric. There are plenty of things I can do on my own, but manhandling something that large isn't one of them. It's no different than asking for help getting a Christmas tree in and out of my cottage."

When we exited the vet, big wet flakes were falling. Visibility was poor, and there was very little conversation as we traveled home. I texted Wendy and Peter the success story about the animals, and they were both surprised to learn that Watson was with the two dogs. Ellie got much the same reaction when she texted her son and daughter-in-law, plus a bit more.

Matthew called his mother. "Mum, you are where? What are you doing out in this weather?"

"Tsk, tsk, dear. It's been a grand adventure. I've been to Little Rissington, Kingham, and Stow. Have you gotten all the sheep to the barn?"

"Yes, and don't try to change the subject. From what I hear, the road from Bourton is in bad shape, and parts of Astonbury are impassable. Call me if you run into any trouble or as soon as you get home. Honestly, Mum."

I put my hand on Ellie's shoulder. "It's times like this I'm glad Dave is in New York. He'd have the same reaction as Matthew if he had any clue about the weather."

That prompted me to text Dave that we'd found the wanderers and that I'd call him when I arrived home with them. We had already passed Peter's garage, where I saw the lights on in his flat upstairs, and we were approaching the entrance to the Olde Mill Inn. It was hard to tell with the snow falling, but it appeared they didn't have any guests. Everyone must have canceled because of the storm.

Dickens put his paws on the window as we passed the donkey barn. "Martha and Dylan must be inside. No carrots for them today."

Ric slowed the car as we came to the narrow bridge across the River Elfe onto Schoolhouse Lane. "It looks as though we'll have to take the next bridge into the village. We're not going to be able to get across this one."

Ellie leaned forward and peered out the window. As Ric made the left toward the second bridge, she put her hands on the dashboard. "Oh bother, this one's impassable too. When I do make it home, Matthew is never going to let me forget this."

Ric drove slowly down the road toward the next bridge in the hope we could make it across that one. We had no idea what we'd do if we couldn't.

We were still several miles away when Ellie cried, "Stop."

If I'd been driving, I likely would have slammed on the brakes and skidded off the road, but Ric carefully slowed to a stop abreast of an aqua and white van with its nose against a stone wall and its tail partly on the road. Ellie put her hand on Ric's arm and motioned him to drive on and pull over in front of the van.

"Now what?" Ric asked.

I put my hand on Ellie's shoulder. "Ellie, we need to keep moving. We can snap a picture of the license plate and text it to Jonas."

She turned to look at me. "There's no harm in looking in the van. If it's the right one, there could be evidence in it."

"I do *not* believe I'm hearing this. If it's the right one, the dognappers could be in it or somewhere nearby. This is a bad move."

She pulled a flashlight from the glove box and opened her door. "Did you see anyone in it? I didn't. Come on, this won't take long."

"Ric, wait here," I said as I followed her.

When I reached her side, I grasped her arm. "Ellie, hold on. Do you hear whimpering? Stay here and give me the light. Let me look."

I crept to the driver's side window and peeked inside. No one was in the front seat. I stepped back to look in the middle section. In the small beam of light, I saw three dogs curled up in a heap. I wasn't good with dog breeds, but I thought one was a Jack Russell and perhaps another was a Yorkie. When they let loose with high-pitched barks, I thought of Henry. He called small dogs like these yappers.

Whispering to Ellie to join me, I tugged on one of the double doors on the side and jumped when it opened with a loud creak. I hadn't opened it wide enough for the interior light to come on, or maybe it wasn't working.

By my side, Ellie gasped. "Oh, my goodness, look at them. They must be frozen, Leta. We've got to get them out of there. Just wait until I get my hands on the people who left them here."

I was more worried about those people getting their hands on us. "Ellie, I'll stay here. You get Ric and some towels. We need to wrap them in something so they don't get away from us."

She trudged to the Land Rover. I heard her speaking to Ric and saw the light come on when she opened the boot to get the towels. Curious as to what lay beyond the wall, I worked my way to the other side of the van. I kept one hand on the wall and shone the light on the ground as I walked. I was too short to see over the wall, but I thought I heard animals—not dogs, maybe sheep or cows. Could there be a barn behind it?

It didn't matter. What was most important now was to rescue the dogs. As I turned to retrace my steps, a hand grabbed my hood and yanked me back. I let out a yelp and fell to the ground, dropping my flashlight. A hand clamped over my mouth, as a voice hissed, "What are you doing?"

It wasn't like I could answer with his hand over my mouth, but he didn't seem to care. His other arm went around my waist, and he jerked me to my feet. Holding me tight against his chest, he backed along the wall, muttering obscenities all the way.

He was tall, and he had to be strong because my feet didn't touch the ground as he carried me along. He seemed impervious to my flailing arms and legs as I tried to elbow and kick him. When I pulled off my gloves and scratched his face, he grabbed my right hand and bit down hard.

At my yelp, he grasped my chin and twisted my head. I tried to avoid his foul alcohol-laden breath but froze when he slurred the words, "You'll pay for that, you stupid cow."

As warm blood trickled down my fingers, I stuffed my freezing hands in my pockets. I was digging through a wad of tissues when my injured hand grazed my smooth egg-shaped key chain. Digging it out of my pocket, I pulled the pin.

Almost simultaneously, the siren pierced the air, a powerful flashlight beam hit my eyes, and my attacker dropped me. I stumbled forward and took off, running headlong into Ric, who was holding the flashlight. The next thing I heard was the sound of a shotgun blast followed by Ellie shouting, "Don't tempt me."

I turned to see a giant of a man caught in the beam of the flashlight. Leaning against the wall with his hands over his ears, he garbled words I couldn't make out.

Ric handed me the flashlight and tugged the key chain from my fingers. When he stuck the pin in it and silenced the alarm, I breathed a sigh of relief and sagged against him.

"Constable James?" Ellie said. "Are you still there? We've got at least one of the scoundrels, and there may be more."

Looking from Ellie to Ric, I tried to understand what was happening. "What, where?"

"She's talking on her Bluetooth, Leta. I wasn't taking any chances. I called Constable James as soon as you two left the car, and Ellie put her earpiece in when she came back for towels. Good thing too."

"But the shotgun? Where was the shotgun?"

Holding the gun steady on the man, who was now slumped against the wall, Ellie chuckled. "I stowed it beneath the blankets. It pays to be prepared." *A shotgun? An earpiece? Who is this woman?*

Ric put a shovel in my free hand. We'd brought it in case we got stuck in the snow. "If he moves, feel free to wallop him, Leta. I think that's preferable to Ellie shooting him. I'm going to check the Land Rover for rope. Ellie thinks there may be some in the boot. Let's hope there is."

Moving to my side, Ellie cradled the shotgun in one arm as she looked me over. "Leta, are you okay? Did he hurt you?"

I wiggled my hand. "Only my fingers. What are we going to do? It will take ages for Jonas to get here, if he can make it at all."

"No worries, dear. Gemma had the presence of mind to call Peter. He's got snow tires on his tow truck, and he's just down the road."

When my attacker started to stand, Ellie stopped him. "I'd hate for my finger to slip, young man. Now, why don't you tell us who you are."

He could barely get his name out. "Lurch. They call me Lurch."

A nervous giggle escaped my mouth. "I was attacked by Lurch? From the Addams Family? And is your partner Uncle Fester?"

Just then, headlights blinded me. Peter pulled up, slammed the door, and made his way past the van to where we stood. He was carrying a tire iron and stopped halfway to us. "Um, Ellie, do you think you could lower the shotgun?"

"Since you asked so nicely, I will. And now that you're here, I don't think I'll need it."

Peter stood guard over Lurch as I watched in a daze. I knew Ric had reached the Land Rover when I heard Dickens. "Leta, I'm coming."

My delayed shock took over as my friends swung into action. Ric and Peter secured Lurch's hands and feet and tied him to a tree for good measure. Ellie stowed her shotgun in the boot and returned to wrap the small dogs in towels. We tucked the three shivering bodies next to Buttercup.

Dickens's protective Pyr genes kicked in as he leaped in and settled next to them. "I'll keep them warm, Leta."

Ellie was all business as she draped a blanket over my shoulders. "Here, Leta, your lips are blue. Are you sure you're okay?"

All I could do was nod and lean against the bumper. In the distance, I saw Peter following the stone wall. He disappeared for a moment and then called to Ric. "I've found a gate. Bring the shovel, and let's check this out."

The phrase about taking a knife to a gunfight entered my mind, as I wondered whether a tire iron and shovel would be sufficient. When the two returned, dragging a man between them, I had my answer. They tied their captive to the tree next to Lurch.

Peter came around the van. "Looks as though they broke into the cottage and helped themselves to the whiskey. This one was passed out with a bottle in his hand. Tried their hands at building a fire, but it's not much more than a smokey mess. They should be thankful you came along before they froze."

Ellie laughed, but I couldn't manage more than a weak smile.

Giving me a concerned look, Peter continued. "I think that does it, ladies. Any word about how soon the police will be here?"

As though his question had conjured the constabulary, headlights appeared from the direction of the High Street bridge. Constable James was accompanied by another officer, and the two took charge, searching the van first. Once they moved on to the cottage, Peter positioned his tow truck and hooked up the van.

I watched numbly as the police transferred the prisoners to the car and then conferred with Peter, Ellie, and Ric. When they nodded and moved in different directions, I assumed a decision had been made. The police car pulled away, Ellie and Ric returned to the Land Rover, and Peter came to my side.

He put his arm around me and nudged me toward his truck. "Constable James says he had a report that the far bridge is impassable too, so I'm calling Gavin and we're all going to the inn."

When Gavin answered, he confirmed there were no guests. "We'll have a sleepover! Isn't that what you Americans call it, Leta?"

Giving it my all, I tried to perk up. "Yes, or a slumber party or a pajama party. I hope Libby can outfit me and Ellie."

When our two vehicles made it to the inn, Gavin greeted us out front and directed us to the side entrance so we could leave our coats and snow-covered boots. He took one look at me and draped the blanket back over my shoulders.

Libby called out as we made our way toward the kitchen, "In here. I've prepared finger sandwiches to tide us over until dinner, and of course, plenty of hot chocolate and tea. We'll serve cocktails in front of the fire later after you've rested." Sinking into a kitchen chair, I gulped tea and nibbled a sandwich and didn't move until Ric and Gavin came through the kitchen with Buttercup, followed by Dickens and Watson.

I trailed after them to the sitting room, where the two men settled Buttercup by the fire with a bowl of water. Her animal companions were having a conversation, but I couldn't make out their soft meows and barks. Dickens answered my unspoken question. "Watson will watch over Buttercup until she starts to snore."

I was looking around for Christie when I heard her. "Where's Leta? I need to see Leta."

Laughing, Ellie walked in with the backpack. "She's been caterwauling the whole way. Even Watson couldn't quiet her down."

When Peter joined us, he handed me a shot glass. "Here, Libby says you need this."

I looked askance at what I assumed was some kind of whiskey, but with Peter's prodding, I drank it. As I leaned my head on the couch back, he took the glass from my hand.

"Um, Leta, what did you do to your hand?"

"Lurch bit it."

"Bloody hell, there's no telling what you could catch from him!" He hopped up and returned with a bottle of disinfectant, cotton balls, and several bandages.

As he cleaned and bandaged my hand, I asked about the dogs we'd rescued. He explained that Libby had provided a basket for the three small dogs and decided to make them comfortable in the toasty laundry room near the dryer.

Patting my shoulder, he stood. "At least you don't need a trip to A&E this time. Now, do you think you and Ellie can stay out of trouble if I go home?"

The dowager countess gave him an amused look and told him to be sure to let Wendy and Belle know all was well.

Soon Gavin assigned us our rooms and offered to carry trays if we wanted to put our feet up and munch upstairs. "You know, we stocked up for weekend guests, and you lot are it. I hope you're hungry."

In the Green Room, I propped myself against the headboard and tucked the blankets around my legs. Watson and Christie lay on either side of me, and Dickens stretched out on the rug, where Paddington joined him. The shot of whiskey had revived me, at least temporarily. "Okay, guys, I have lots of questions. First, Dickens, why did you run off?"

As though he were on stage, he raised himself to a sitting position. "Leta, Buttercup barked and lit out down the road. I thought I could get her to come back, but there was no stopping her."

Watson chimed in. "And when I spied them jogging past the donkey barn, I knew trouble was brewing. It wasn't the first time Buttercup ran off, and she always cried for Tanya when she did."

Moving to my stomach, Christie looked at me. "Tanya's gone like Henry is, right, Leta? Why is Buttercup so confused?"

"Not sure, princess, but we'll have to keep a close watch on her. Now, Dickens, did Buttercup seem to know where she was going?"

"Oh yes. She called it home or Tanya's home, and she never hesitated. She knew."

Buttercup's escorts explained that they sometimes traveled on the verge but more often across fields. Watson knew the best places to find handouts, as he often wandered nearly to Bourton on his nightly jaunts. If a kindly person didn't respond to his plaintive meows, they'd find a garbage can with a loose lid. They didn't go hungry very often.

Paddington head-butted Dickens. "Punky saw you in Bourton. Did you get fish and chips?"

Dickens licked his lips, and I imagined he was savoring the memory. *My boy and food.*

He returned to the story and explained that he trotted by Buttercup's right side, especially when they were near a road, because she was blind in her right eye. He was like a guard rail keeping her from veering off.

Hearing Watson describe his habit of checking out the terrain ahead or bringing up the rear made me smile. "Watson, you were not only the advance scout but also the rear guard. I guess Buttercup was the navigator."

Christie nudged the tabby. "Weren't you cold? Where did you sleep?"

He playfully batted her nose. "Me, cold? Nope. When we were moving, we stayed warm, and most nights Dickens and Buttercup dug beneath the leaf cover to make a bed, and we three slept close together. Dickens slept in a shed one night."

"I know he did, Watson. Now, who's going to tell me how he escaped the shed? Mr. Pike says the door was latched."

Dickens stood and put his paws on the bed. "Watson's a smart cat. Tell her, Watson."

The handsome tabby preened. "It was easy. I leaped to the window box closest to the latch and pushed the top piece back. It took a few tries, but it finally worked, and Dickens pushed the door open. We tried to get Buttercup to join us inside, but she wouldn't go near any buildings. I think she was scared."

"She was, Leta. She was worried someone would keep her from getting to Tanya. Watson and I tried to tell her that Tanya wasn't there anymore, but she wouldn't listen."

Buttercup's companions hoped that once she reached her old home, she would understand. They thought she had to see for herself. When I asked about Lucy, Watson explained that Buttercup whined both their names as she slept.

The last leg of the journey was difficult because Buttercup stepped in a hole and did something to her paw, but she limped along, determined to make it to her old home. She barked at the cottage door and the door to the shed until she finally gave up and drug herself into her doghouse.

Dickens nudged my hand. "It was sad, Leta. She barked, 'Where's Tanya?' and laid her head on her paws."

I wondered aloud what would have happened if I hadn't figured out what was going on. Dickens had a ready answer to that question. "Leta, I knew you would find us. You wouldn't let us stay lost."

Christie tied a bow around the tale. "Dickens is our little hero dog, and now, Leta, you're the little hero girl."

Chuckling, I assured the menagerie that I might be little but that I was no longer a girl. "How about the little hero lady?"

I was about to drift off when Libby knocked on the door and called, "Leta, may I come in?"

When I invited her in, she looked around the room. "I hesitated to knock because I thought you were on the phone, but the longer I listened . . . well,

I could have sworn you were holding court with the animals."

Chuckling, I made light of her comment. "Of course, I was, Libby, just like you talk to Paddington."

She handed me a set of flannel pajamas and a pair of clean socks as I wondered how much she'd heard. I was so accustomed to talking to Dickens and Christie when I was alone with them that I'd lost sight of the fact I wasn't in my bedroom at home. *And soon, Dave will be living with me. I need to be more careful.*

CHAPTER FOURTEEN

AFTER A SHORT DOZE, I washed my face and grabbed a notepad from the bedroom table. I had awakened with an idea and wanted to capture the salient points before I went downstairs to the sitting room. Pleasantly surprised that my writing hand didn't hurt, I scribbled away.

Buttercup yipped a greeting when I entered the room, trailed by three cats and Dickens. "It's warm in here."

Sitting beside her on the rug, Ric rubbed her head. "I think she's doing well. She wandered to the kitchen for a bite, and she seems happy to see her friends."

It was a comfy setting. The fireplace was flanked by floor-to-ceiling bookshelves, and overstuffed easy chairs were arranged around it. We could enjoy the warmth of the fire and watch the snowfall through the French doors at the end of the room. Gavin handed me a glass of red wine. "Drink up. No one's going anywhere tonight."

Before I could take a sip, Ellie raised her glass and cleared her throat. "I'd say today's adventure deserves a toast. Here's to Leta for having the idea to check Buttercup's old home in Kingham. Goodness knows what would have happened to our traveling trio if she hadn't."

I raised my glass next. "There's plenty of praise to go around. It was a team effort, Ellie. Here's to you for providing the vehicle *and* the shotgun. And here I thought rescuing Dickens and Buttercup was enough of an adventure."

Her eyes twinkled. "Stumbling across the dognappers was a bonus, don't you think?"

Ric and I exchanged glances. "What I think is we're very fortunate it turned out the way it did. I mean, I hate to be a party pooper, but what if they'd been armed?"

"But they weren't. Except for Lurch chewing on your fingers, things turned out rather well. And Ric, many thanks for your assistance. Not only were you an excellent chauffeur in difficult circumstances, you were also quite adept at hog-tying our prisoner. Do I even want to know where you learned how to do that?"

Ric blushed and ducked his head. Being in our debt could be the best thing that ever happened to him. Ellie would see to it that Pepper's Pets got the funding it needed, and there was no telling

what other opportunities might come his way. She
seemed to be taking a liking to him.

As she passed a tray of spinach balls and cheese
straws my way, Libby laughed. "While you were
resting, Leta, Ellie gave us the scoop on the
capture of the dognappers. With Ric's color
commentary, it put me in mind of *The Mrs.
Bradley Mysteries*—the ones with Diana Rigg and
the actor from Midsomer Murders as her chauffer.
Except Mrs. Bradley had a Rolls Royce instead of a
Bentley and a Land Rover."

Ellie looked at Ric. "Don't get any ideas—you're
not driving the Bentley."

After my anxiety over the lost dogs and
the afternoon's adventure, the lighthearted
conversation was a delightful diversion. Good
food, good wine, and good friends were a
wonderful combination.

As he refilled our wine glasses, Gavin gave me an
amused look. "So, Leta, Libby tells me you've been

talking to the animals, à la Dr. Dolittle. Did you get the scoop on their journey?"

Thank goodness I was prepared for this eventuality. I knew as soon as I saw Libby's face earlier that she was suspicious. Not that she would ever believe I understood them, but it wouldn't take much for her to worry that I was delusional.

"Well, yes, as a matter of fact, I did. They wanted to keep it a secret, but once I laid out the clues I'd gathered, Dickens and Watson 'fessed up."

Ellie clapped her hands. "Oh, I can't wait to hear this. Is it story-time?"

With a flourish, I pulled out my notepad. "Yes, we need to work on a title, but as befits the founder of the Little Old Ladies' Detective Agency, I believe I've solved the mystery of the traveling trio. Heck, maybe that's the title."

I laid out the sequence of events and the clues. "Before Dickens and Buttercup ever took off, there were indications that she missed Lucy's sister. Lucy

found her sitting in my driveway one day, and
we know Buttercup crossed the river to the inn.
Susan, the stockwoman at the estate, told me that
Buttercup often wandered the river. Also, I'm not
sure when she did it, but I noticed some animal had
been digging beneath the back gate to the estate,
and I think now it must have been Buttercup." *No
need to tell them I got that bit from Basil.*

"Even without those incidents, I think you'd
all agree that it couldn't have been Dickens who
decided to venture off into the great unknown."

As my friends concurred with my conclusion,
Dickens barked, "Of course, it wasn't me. I told
you. I had to take care of Buttercup."

"In the beginning, I didn't put all that together or
connect those incidents to the fact that Buttercup's
owner had died not long ago. All I had to go on
were the sightings of Dickens and Buttercup. Little
did any of us know that Watson was with those
two."

Ric rose from his cross-legged position by Buttercup and put his hand on the mantel. *How does he do that in one graceful move?* "I remember, Leta, we discounted the sighting in Clapton because someone had seen Dickens on the road to Bourton."

"That's right. A nurse on her way to work saw a white dog near the bridge over the River Elfe. And the next sighting was in Little Rissington. The kind soul who saw them there fed them, but couldn't get them to come near his cottage. Add to that what I read on the internet about dogs traveling as far as fourteen miles a day, and I didn't know what to do. I had no idea where they were headed."

Paddington meowed, "Don't forget that Punky saw them in Bourton."

Ignoring Paddington, I continued. "Dave and I debated whether Buttercup might be looking for Lucy. We didn't think about Tanya. And then the call came in from Charlie Pike in Idbury. And, oh, by the way, no one had seen Watson in days."

"If only Mr. Pike had let you fetch them Thursday night," Ellie said, "Buttercup might not have been injured, and we wouldn't have been out in this weather. I guess, though, we don't know when she sprained her paw, and it was certainly a grand adventure today."

Again, I had no intention of letting on that I knew the details and timing of Buttercup's injury. "It's funny how things happen. It was flipping through the copy of *The Incredible Journey* that made me wonder whether Watson was with the two dogs. And no doubt it was falling asleep with that thought in my head that triggered the idea that Buttercup was headed to her old home. It didn't matter whether she was searching for Tanya or Lucy."

The corners of Ellie's mouth lifted. "And this is why you're our fearless leader. You contacted Lucy for the name of the village and off we went."

Ric chuckled. "Did they happen to tell you how they opened the shed door?"

"They didn't exactly say, but I think Watson did what Tao did in *The Incredible Journey*. I can see him pushing the latch up with his paw."

Dickens barked. "Don't you remember? He told you that's what he did!"

"You know," mused Ellie, "he's forever breaking into the cupboards at home, so that fits."

Tilting her head, Libby studied me. "Didn't I hear you say something about a little hero girl when I came to your bedroom door? And, by the way, do you always talk to yourself when you're mapping out clues?"

"Only when I don't have Ellie or Belle or Wendy to talk to. I stare into space and think aloud as I jot down ideas." Letting her think I talked to myself was better than the alternative.

"So, what was that bit about a hero girl?"

"I thought about Dickens's tag, the one Kirsten gave him after he rescued us—gosh, was that only a few months ago? His tag says 'Dickens the Hero Dog,' though Kirsten called him the *little* hero dog. I was imagining Dickens and Watson thinking I was their hero." I looked at Dickens. "I'm your hero, right, Dickens?"

When he barked, "Yes, you are," and came to my side, we all laughed.

I raised my glass. "And, that my friends, concludes the Mystery of the Traveling Trio."

We enjoyed a hearty meal of soup and home-baked rolls followed by cookies Jill had made that morning before Libby sent her home. I was the first to climb the stairs, eager to change into flannel pajamas and call Dave. It was a lengthy conversation, as he wanted to hear the details of the journey to Idbury and insisted I repeat the Mystery of the Traveling Trio the way I'd told it in the sitting room.

"That's quite a tale, Leta. I know it's more of a story than a column, but I bet your newspaper readers over here would enjoy it."

"You know, I think you're right, and for sure, the *Astonbury Aha* readers would get a kick out of it. With all the alerts about missing dogs, they're bound to enjoy a story with a happy ending."

"And you're home safe and sound now?"

"Um, we actually wound up at the inn because we couldn't get across the bridge to Schoolhouse Lane. We're having a spend-the-night party."

"Of course you are. It's part of the LOL process that you party after you solve a mystery, isn't it? Well Tuppence, it looks like you've done it again. Now, get some rest, and we'll talk tomorrow. Love you."

I told myself I would have shared the rest of the story if he'd given me a chance. But I was exhausted and it was better left for the next day.

The sun was streaming in the window the next morning when I opened my eyes. Glancing at the bedside clock, I realized it was eight a.m. *I can't remember the last time I slept this late, and I can't believe Christie isn't bugging me to get up.*

When I rolled over and stretched, I knew why there wasn't a furball meowing on my chest. I was alone in the Green Room. Someone must have let my animals out and left me sleeping. If I wasn't mistaken, that someone was either Libby or Gavin and they were downstairs making breakfast. I hoped there would be something left by the time I got down there.

My bathroom was set up with a toothbrush, toothpaste, and soap, and soon I felt nearly human.

I dried my hair and put yesterday's clothes on. They would have to do until I could return home. Since it had stopped snowing, maybe it would be today.

Wandering into the kitchen in my stocking feet, I was greeted by Ellie. "Good morning. Do I need to ask how you slept?"

"Like a log. I feel like a new woman. How 'bout you?"

"Quite well, thank you. Ric and Gavin have gone to check on the bridge to Schoolhouse Lane. Hopefully, we'll be able to make it home soon."

As I poured a mug of coffee, Libby came in from the laundry room, followed by Dickens and Paddington. "Good morning. Dickens has been chasing balls and digging in the snow. He's such a happy boy."

"And Paddington, what's he been up to?"

"No good! He continues to see the striped scarves on Raggedy Ann and Andy as cat toys. By the way, Buttercup went outside too. She didn't chase any balls, but she rolled in the snow. I don't think her paw is bothering her."

The morning was off to a good start. I helped myself to bacon and toast from the warming oven and sighed. "It's a wonder how good I feel now that the animals are home. You don't realize how worry can weigh you down."

Libby looked at Ellie. "Have you told her the other news?"

Ellie's eyes sparkled. "Not yet. Guess what?"

"Haven't a clue. What?"

"Thanks to you, the dognappers are behind bars in Stow."

I choked on my coffee. "What do you mean, thanks to me? You're the woman who held one of them at gunpoint, and Ric and Peter found the second one."

"Yes, but Lurch's attack on you allowed the police to charge him with aggravated assault instead of merely stealing a dog. Honestly, something needs to be done about that. It should be classified as more than a property crime."

I looked at my bandaged hand. "So glad to be of help."

"And they've also been charged with breaking and entering. We know our misguided petty thieves slid their van into a wall last night, but they also broke into the unoccupied cottage it fronted. I mean, I assumed they had, but the police had to locate the owners to confirm the two weren't guests. And leaving those poor dogs in the van? That and the several dog collars found in the police search of the vehicle sealed the deal.

"Just think, Leta, if we hadn't bumped into Ric, we wouldn't have known about the van. We never would have paid any attention to it on the side of the road."

She winked at me, and I got the message that we weren't sharing the Ric story with Libby. She was right. Without Ric and his altruistic scheme, the dognappers might have gotten away scot-free.

I laughed. "Is it appropriate to toast with a cup of coffee? Cheers to you and Belle. You deserve plenty of credit for uncovering the ransom plot and the setup at the cricket pavilion."

As we clinked mugs, I whispered in her ear, "And for twigging—I love that word—to the connection between lost dog alerts and Ric's anonymous notes."

Ellie chuckled. "It's been quite a week, hasn't it? Between the Canine Caper and the Mystery of the Traveling Trio, we've had plenty of excitement. Whatever will we do for the rest of the month?"

CHAPTER FIFTEEN

COMMANDEERING GAVIN'S COMPUTER IN the conservatory, I composed a detailed email to friends and family about the return of Dickens and Buttercup. The subject line was "The Mystery of the Traveling Trio," and I was getting quite attached to it. *It's the perfect title for a column.*

I turned my gaze to the sparkling winter scene visible through the windows. A cardinal sat on the birdhouse roof as though surveying his domain.

The first to respond to my email was Lucy, and she did it via phone. "Good morning, Leta. I know we texted about the rescue last night, but this email has much more detail. I'm so grateful that you figured it out. How's Buttercup's paw today?"

"She's been out to play in the snow, and I think she'll have that bandage off soon. Will you be able to make it back today?"

"I'm at the Paris airport now about to depart for Heathrow. Beyond that, it's iffy. I'd rather spend the night in London than take the train to Moreton-on-Marsh and get stuck there. I'll check the weather after I land."

After I assured her Buttercup would be well taken care of, she promised to keep me updated on her plans. Christie wandered in and leaped into my lap. "You haven't given Dickens his talking-to yet. You will, won't you? He better not ever leave us again."

I was hesitant to respond in case someone heard me, so I whispered. "I'll do it when we get home."

So far, there had been no further comments about my talking to the animals, and I hoped it would stay that way.

The sound of tires crunching on snow disturbed the peaceful morning, and I soon heard voices in the foyer. I expected to see Gavin and Ric, but it was Wendy who stuck her head into the conservatory. Attired in a baby blue parka, matching leggings, and a blue knit cap, she was a cheerful sight.

"Well, aren't you something? You look as though you're ready for a photo shoot. All we need is a pond for ice skating."

"Not on your life. The last time I went ice skating, I fell flat on my bum."

"Do I hear your mum?"

"Yes, Peter brought us over. When Mum heard the van story from Peter and the traveling trio story from Libby, she was determined to get it straight from you and Ellie, so she called Peter first thing this morning and badgered him into picking us up. The roads aren't clear, but they're better."

Unzipping her parka, she plopped on a chair in front of Gavin's desk. "I hear Ric was a real asset. I think we made the right decision about him, don't you?"

"For sure. Have you heard that Jonas has charged the dognappers?"

"No! I was hopeful but didn't know for sure."

"Let's head to the kitchen and get Ellie to tell that story. You know, at the rate Ellie and your mum are going, I wouldn't be surprised if they opened a new arm of the Little Old Ladies' Detective Agency."

We were just in time to hear a cork pop. Holding a bottle of champagne, Libby turned to us with a grin. "Do you know how long it's been since Ellie, Belle, and I have had time to just sit and talk? This snowstorm is like an early Christmas present."

The three were long-time friends, but Libby was so busy with the inn she rarely had a chance to accompany Belle and Ellie on their outings. Listening to their chatter and laughter was a joy.

As Libby prepared a pitcher of mimosas, Ellie suggested we start with The Mystery of the Traveling Trio. I had an attentive audience, and my listeners seemed quite taken with the tale. Ellie followed it with the more serious story of how the dognappers wound up behind bars.

Peter quietly sipped his drink as the stories unfolded. When Ellie finished her story, he caught my eye. "And just think, you incurred only one minor injury in the process."

When Gavin and Ric arrived with the news that the road to Schoolhouse Lane was clear, they found a tipsy group of revelers. Libby hugged her husband and handed him a champagne flute. "Do they have to go? I was hoping they'd be snowed in for another night."

Ellie insisted on taking Buttercup home with her, and when she and Ric dropped me off, I was thankful that Ric offered to build me a fire. Once they were safely on their way, I changed into leggings and Henry's old Georgia Tech sweatshirt and promptly fell asleep on the couch.

When I rolled over hours later, the sun was setting. Dickens lay snoring on the hearth, and Christie was on her back beside him with all four paws in the air. I yawned and stretched and reached to tickle her belly.

"Are you glad he's home?"

"Yes, and he promised not to run off again—ever."

Christie was a sassy, demanding thing, but beneath her feisty exterior, she was a sweetheart. When she followed me to the kitchen, I knew she was ready for a dab of wet food. Unbelievably, she ate it without complaint—no disdainful looks or snooty comments about fluffing it. *My, my, will wonders never cease?*

I was sipping lavender tea when Constable James knocked on my door. "Jonas, come in, come in. Would you like a cup of tea?"

He looked done in, and when he told me he was off duty, I settled him in front of the fire and offered him a sandwich. He wolfed it down and then leaned his head against the back of the sofa. "I know you're glad to have Dickens home, Leta, and you and the Little Old Ladies made three more dog owners happy too. I wanted to stop by to tell you how grateful they are."

"All the credit goes to the two senior members of the team. They were especially pleased with themselves, you know."

"As well they should be. I felt like Santa when I called the owners of the three dogs you found. They were overjoyed to hear their dogs were safe and sound, and they've all paid a visit to the inn to get their pets. And the good news is that when I followed up on the loose tags from the van, I found that all those dogs were already home. Not before their owners paid a ransom, but they were home."

I couldn't wait to tell Belle and Ellie. The news made me think of Ellie's remark about a happy holiday for some little boy or girl.

"And, Leta, you'll love this. When I questioned the owners who'd paid a ransom, it turned out several had noticed an aqua and white van around the time their dogs went missing. I was able to match those locations with break-ins that had occurred in the vicinity. These two plonkers will do time—not nearly enough, but some."

"Jonas, what do you know about them? Did they just decide that the Cotswolds were a prime spot or what?"

He ran his hand through his hair. "They're cousins—one failed out of university and the other was out of a job. It was a distant cousin, part of a gang in Yorkshire, who gave them the idea. I had no idea that dognapping is as common there as it is in London. With the ransom money and the burglaries, they had visions of building a criminal empire. Stupid sods."

"And DCI Burton? Is he pleased?"

"He is now, but not before he tore into DI Taylor and threatened to discipline me and her both. Said she never should have let me spend time on the case. It didn't matter that it was my own time. She took the heat for me, and now he's taking the credit for collaring a burglary ring. Can you believe it?"

Sadly, I could.

"Anyway, the best I can tell, there's no one else operating in the area now. That's not to say someone won't take the place of these two, but for now, we're good. By the way, while you were working on this, did you turn up anything about the strange notes with the letters pasted on them? The two masterminds sitting in the cell in Stow deny all knowledge of those."

This is dangerous territory. "We found out that all those owners had their dogs returned safe and sound, so we're looking at it as all's well that ends well."

He shook his head. "True, and if it makes those owners more careful, maybe it's a good thing."

Seeing his eyes at half-mast, I knew it was time to send him on his way. And it was time for me to call Dave. I'd delayed telling him the rest of the story for as long as I could.

He was packing when I called. "At this rate, I'll be able to ship most of the books before I fly over for Christmas. There's not much left to pack after that. So, is Dickens happy to be home?"

"Yes, and if you can believe it, Christie even curled up with him this afternoon. Of course, he still needs a bath, but that will have to wait until Posh Pets opens Monday."

We had our usual conversation about this and that, and when there was a pause, I broached the other subject.

"I have good news about the dognappers. Jonas hauled them in last night, and he dropped by here a little while ago to give me an update."

"Based on what you told me, I assume they'll be out in no time, right?"

When I didn't answer right away, he knew something was up. "Leta? What is it?"

"Well, actually, Ellie and I kind of stumbled across them, and that's how Jonas was able to arrest them."

He groaned, and I pictured him running his hands through his hair. "Why does that sound ominous?"

I took him through the part about Ric's sighting of the aqua and white Volkswagen van and us not being able to cross the bridge to Astonbury. "It was when we were on our way to the farthest bridge that Ellie spotted the van on the side of the road and told Ric to pull over. I told her it was a bad idea."

"I'd have to agree with you on that. So, what exactly happened?"

He didn't even let me get to the worst part before he said, "You what? You traipsed through the snow, with your knee?"

If only that was all there was to it. "My knee is fine. It's only my fingers that got hurt."

This must be what people mean when they say, the silence spoke volumes. I took a deep breath and rattled off the next bit. "This big guy grabbed me, but I had your alarm, and I set it off, and Ellie shot her gun in the air, and it all worked out fine."

I didn't have to see him. I could picture his lips set in a grim line. "Leta, do you hear yourself? Why? Why do you have to put yourself in danger?"

He didn't want to hear that it was Ellie, not me. Every time I said *but*, he spoke over me. I'd heard these same admonishments before and couldn't argue with them. Maybe I didn't set out to put myself in danger, but somehow that's where I always wound up.

"But, Dave, this time, it *really* was different. I thought all I had to worry about was getting stuck in the snow while trying to find Dickens. I didn't even know about the van until we were on the way to Kingham."

At least he didn't say that what we did was *stupid*, though I knew it was. The one time he'd used that word with me, I'd hung up on him. And that escapade in Tintagel hadn't been my fault either. It was Wendy's idea.

When he finally ran out of steam, I asked, "How long am I going to be in the doghouse?"

He sighed. "I hate it when we argue."

"So do I. And, yes, I know this is pretty much the only thing we argue about."

"And I know you're not going to change, no matter what I say or do."

He was right. And what did that say about us—about our relationship? My next words came out as a whisper. "Dave, are you still coming?"

"For Christmas? Of course, I am."

"And after that? Are you—are you still moving in?"

"What? How can you ask me that? Of course, I'm moving in. Couples argue, and this won't be the last time we do. Didn't you and Henry argue?"

I gulped. "Yes, and somehow we always worked things out. We compromised."

"And so will we. You'll keep being you. You'll keep making me crazy, and I'll keep worrying about you. That doesn't change a thing. Except that when we argue, it will be face to face." He paused. "And that means we get to make up face to face." I was sure I detected a smile in that last line.

CHAPTER SIXTEEN

I<small>T WAS</small> D<small>ECEMBER</small> 23<small>RD</small>, and I was back at the Moreton-on-Marsh train station waiting for Dave. This would be our first Christmas together. Last year, I'd spent it with my Astonbury friends, and Dave had joined me in time for us to enjoy New Year's Eve in London. It had been early in our relationship. This year, we'd have a quiet December holiday, and come January 2nd, he'd return to New York City to finish packing for his mid-January move to my cottage. I wondered how long it would be before we began to refer to it as *our* cottage.

I thought of myself as a glass-half-full person—except, perhaps, when it came to romance. I'd had my share of relationships before I married Henry, and my heart had been broken more than once. His sudden death had nearly undone me. He was the man I thought I'd grow old with, and I hadn't looked at another man until I met Dave.

He claimed he was attracted to me the moment he set eyes on me, and though I didn't expect to be asked out, I was delighted when I was. We had an immediate connection, a spark, but I told myself it was just a date. After all, he was visiting from across the pond. Nothing would come of it beyond a few pleasant hours. But something did.

And here we were, fifteen months later. Dave didn't propose marriage, but he *did* propose giving up his life in New York City to join me in

Astonbury. I was ecstatic, and I was anxious, and I was trying to take it one day at a time—a difficult approach for a planner like me. We'd never been together for more than a month at a time, and we'd spent months apart between visits. How would living together work out?

I was deep in thought and would have missed Dave emerging from the station if not for Dickens. "He's here, Leta. Dave's here."

Throwing the door open, I jogged toward him. When we met in the middle of the parking lot, he dropped his bags, held his arms wide, and lifted me off my feet. "Merry Christmas, Tuppence."

How I love this man. "Merry Christmas, sweetheart."

Our routine when he arrived was to grab a bite in Stow or Bourton before making the short drive to Astonbury. Once there, Dave would shower while I stoked the fire and busied myself downstairs. The one unknown was whether he would lie down for what was supposed to be a quick nap or join me. Today, the nap won out. After an hour, I climbed the stairs. He was asleep on his side with Christie tucked against his stomach and Dickens on the rug. I climbed into the bed, snuggled against his back, and draped my arm over his side.

I was alone when I woke to the faint sound of a Mannheim Steamroller Christmas song. In the kitchen, Dave was preparing a plate of hummus, cheese, and crackers. He'd gotten pretty good at finding his way around my kitchen, though he'd yet to cook a meal in it from scratch. In his minuscule kitchen in New York, he made a mean chili and could throw together a variety of stir-fry dishes. Other than toasting bagels, that was about it. He was no different from Henry in that regard.

He poured two glasses of red wine and handed one to me. "Here's to Christmas in the Cotswolds."

We spent Christmas Eve day close to home. We visited Toby's Tearoom for hot chocolate and shopped the Book Nook. Alike in our belief that one could never have too many books, we came home with several. A walk to feed the donkeys was a must, as was an early evening visit to the village green to see the tree.

In unspoken agreement, we dressed up for our meal—no jeans for Christmas Eve. Dave wore the black sweater I'd given him last Christmas, and I topped my black velveteen leggings with a red silk top. I set the table with the new place mats I'd found at the tree lighting and prepared a simple but elegant dinner of pork tenderloin roasted with cubed sweet potatoes and glazed with maple syrup. Basil green beans and a salad completed the main course, and we topped it off with kourbiades served with coffee and amaretto in the sitting room.

We sipped our liqueur in front of the glowing fire as Christmas music played softly in the background. "Dave, what's your family tradition? Do you open presents on Christmas Eve or Christmas Day?"

"Growing up, it was always Christmas Day, but now, it's whenever we're together—sometimes the day, and sometimes Christmas Eve. You?"

"Mom and Dad were strict Christmas Day adherents until I was in my teens. Then they gave in and allowed us to open one present each on Christmas Eve. I was wondering what our tradition will be."

"I think I like Christmas Eve. Sitting in front of the fireplace with the candles glowing on the mantel and the tree alight in front of the window? It seems like a festive finish to the evening. What do you think?"

"I like it. You can't beat the candlelight and the tree glowing in the dark. One of your packages is under the tree. Why don't you open that first? I have to get the other one from the guest room closet."

"Hmm. Is there a clue in that? I wonder. Well, both of yours are beneath the tree." He knelt and pulled out a gaily wrapped square box with a tag that said, "Lovely Leta," and the one with his name on it. "You go first."

It was a jar of Shalimar crème. "You know I adore Shalimar, but how did you know I was completely out of the crème?"

He smiled. "I'm an honorary member of the LOLs, aren't I? I snooped. Now, what have we here?" He tore into his box and pulled the tissue paper aside. "Aha! I'll have to wear it tomorrow." It was the green fleece pullover I'd found at the tree lighting, with the new Cycling Cider logo. "I want you to open your other present last, so I guess you'll have to head to the guest room."

I wondered what he was up to, but I obliged.
When I returned with the large square object
draped in a sheet, he studied it. "Do I have to
guess?"

"No." I propped it on the ottoman and lifted
the sheet to reveal Lucy's portrait of Dickens and
Christie. When his mouth dropped open, I wasn't
sure whether he was surprised or disappointed, but
the laugh that followed told me what I needed to
know.

"Will you look at that? It's the dynamic duo. It
even captures their personalities. I swear Christie
has a bossy look on her face, and Dickens is tilting
his head as if to say, 'I want to see the donkeys.'"

"I'm glad you approve. It's Lucy's work."

"It's perfect. Where are we going to hang it?"

"In the office, I think. Unless we hang it on the
wall in the stairway."

"I like the office. There's better light in there."
He looked around for the subjects of the painting.
"What do you say, guys? The office?"

Dickens was comatose by the fire, but Christie
gave her stamp of approval. "Of course, that way I
can see myself from the desk."

"Decision made. The office it is."

I propped it against the easy chair while he moved
to the tree to retrieve his final gift for me. It was
a narrow jeweler's box wrapped in red shiny paper
with a silver bow. The tag read, "To Tuppence
from Dave and Dickens." I gasped with delight
when I opened the hinged box to see a white gold
charm bracelet with one charm. "A charm bracelet?
Do you know I must be the only girl I know who
never had one?"

I pulled it from the box and held it to the light.
The charm was a medallion with the words "My
Little Hero Girl" inscribed above a tiny diamond

chip. "How did you know? I didn't tell you that part, did I?"

"No, but Wendy did when I called her for input on what the first charm should be. Something about Libby hearing you talking to Dickens. By then, I'd looked at so many charms, my eyes were glazing over. I heard the words little hero girl, and I pictured Dickens's medallion. That was all it took."

As I turned it over in my hand, I saw that there was another inscription on the back. I fumbled for my red reading glasses. "You are the joy in my world."

"And you, Dave Prentiss, are the magic in mine."

With my head on his shoulder, we sat in companionable silence until he gave me a lingering kiss and pulled me to my feet. "Shall I tend to Dickens? While you get ready for bed? I think it's time for visions of sugar plums and all that, don't you?"

Blowing out the candles, I gave him a knowing look. "All that? Are you picturing yourself in a cap and me in a kerchief and flannel gown?"

When he clutched his heart in mock horror, I chuckled. "I didn't think so."

Joy, magic, laughs, love. As I laid my long silk nightgown on the bed, I glimpsed my reflection in the mirror. The sparkle in my eyes and my smile said it all. It was beginning to look a lot like Christmas.

BOOK IX

Everything's going according to plan. A new chapter in Dave and Leta's relationship. Publicity tours for Dave's new book. What's not in the plan is murder!

Can the Little Old Ladies read between the lines to discover who wrote the victim's final fatal chapter?

Read ***Pawprints, Prose & Murder*** to find out. Available on Amazon https://amzn.to/3Syid6y

What was Leta's life like before she retired to the Cotswolds?

How did Dickens & Christie become part of the family? Find out in ***Paws, Claws & Mischief***, the prequel to the Dickens & Christie mystery series.

Sign up for my newsletter **https://bit.ly/Pennnewsletter** to get your complimentary copy and to learn when the next book is on the way.

Don't miss out on the Dickens & Christie prequel.

If you're new to the series, be sure to check out the earlier books—all available on **Amazon** as ebooks, paperbacks, large print paperbacks, and as downloads through Kindle Unlimited.

Psst ... Please take a minute

Dear Reader,

Writers put their hearts and souls into every book. Nothing makes it more worthwhile than reader reviews. Yes, authors appreciate reviews that provide helpful insights.

If you enjoyed this book, Kathy would love it if you could find the time to leave a good, honest review ... because after everything is said and done, authors write to bring enjoyment to their readers.

Thank you,
Dickens

BOLOGNESE SAUCE RECIPE

Ingredients

- 1 tbsp olive oil

- 3 garlic cloves, minced

- 1 small onion, finely chopped

- 1 lb ground beef or 50/50 ground beef and ground pork

- 24 oz. pureed tomato

- ½ cup water

- 1 tsp each dried basil, oregano, sugar

- 1 tsp fennel seeds optional

- ¼ tsp cayenne pepper

- 1 tsp paprika

1. 1 tsp each salt and pepper or to taste

Instructions

1. Heat oil in a large skillet over high heat.

2. Add onion and garlic and cook for 2 minutes or until onion is translucent.

3. Add meat and cook, breaking it up as you go.

4. When it is just cooked, add fennel, cayenne pepper, paprika, and salt and pepper, and cook for 2 minutes. If you use 93% lean ground beef, you will not have to drain fat.

5. Add tomato puree, water, basil, oregano, and sugar.

6. Bring to a simmer, reduce heat to low, and

cook for 10 minutes. Adjust salt and pepper to taste.

Books mentioned in Candy Canes, Canines & Crime

- *Spenser series* (Robert B. Parker)

- *Sunny Randall series* (Robert B. Parker)

- *How to Find Love in a Bookshop* (Veronica Henry)

- *Rebecca* (Daphne du Maurier)

- *The World According to Garp* (John Irving)

- *The Incredible Journey* (Sheila Burnford)

- *Lucky Boy* (Susan Boase)

- *The Dog Who Rescues Cats* (Leonard Fleischer and Philip Gonzalez)

About the Author

A corporate escapee, Kathy Manos Penn went from crafting change communications to plotting page-turners. She adheres to the adage to "write what you know" and populates her cozy mysteries with well-read, witty senior women, a sassy cat, and a loyal dog. The murders and talking pets, however, exist only in her imagination.

Years ago, when she stumbled onto a side job as a columnist, she saw the opportunity as an entertaining diversion from the corporate grind. Little did she know that her serendipitous foray into writing would lead to a cozy mystery series—much less a 2020 Readers' Favorite Gold Award in the Mystery-Sleuth genre for *Bells, Tails & Murder*, Book I in the series.

Picture her sitting serenely at her desk, surrounded by the four-legged office assistants who inspire the personalities of Dickens & Christie. How does she describe her life? "I'm living a dream I never knew I had."

To learn more about Kathy *and* get a free download of the Dickens & Christie prequel, **sign up** for her newsletter, https://bit.ly/Pennnewsletter .

For book news and pics, follow Kathy on

—Facebook

https://www.facebook.com/KathyManosPennAu

thor/ and

  —Instagram

https://www.instagram.com/kathymanospennau

thor/.

Also By Kathy Manos Penn

Dickens & Christie Mystery Series

Bells, Tails & Murder

Pumpkins, Paws & Murder

Whiskers, Wreaths & Murder

Collectors, Cats & Murder

Castles, Catnip & Murder

Bicycles, Barking & Murder

Pets, Pens & Murder

ON AMAZON

Printed in Great Britain
by Amazon

33654292R10219